Lights! Wedding! Ludhiana!

Dr Jas Kohli is a cosmetic surgeon who, apart from reshaping faces and bodies, is often found aiming his camera at birds and butterflies during the day and gazing dreamily into the sky at night. His emotions often run riot when he sings old Bollywood songs and writing humour is his refuge. He loves life and lemon—squeezing as much as possible from both. This is his third novel.

Reach him at:
Email: drjskohli@gmail.com
Facebook: @AuthorJasKohli
Instagram: @authorjaskohli

Also by the same author:

Lights! Scalpel! Romance!

Lights! Wedding! Ludhiana!

JAS KOHLI

RUPA

Published by
Rupa Publications India Pvt. Ltd 2021
7/16, Ansari Road, Daryaganj
New Delhi 110002

Sales centres:
Allahabad Bengaluru Chennai
Hyderabad Jaipur Kathmandu
Kolkata Mumbai

Copyright © Jas Kohli 2021

This is a work of fiction. Names, characters, places and incidents are either the product of the author's imagination or are used fictitiously and any resemblance to any actual person, living or dead, events or locales is entirely coincidental.

All rights reserved.
No part of this publication may be reproduced, transmitted, or stored in a retrieval system, in any form or by any means, electronic, mechanical, photocopying, recording or otherwise, without the prior permission of the publisher.

ISBN: 978-93-5520-012-9

First impression 2021

10 9 8 7 6 5 4 3 2 1

The moral right of the authors has been asserted.

Printed at Thomson Press India Ltd., Faridabad

This book is sold subject to the condition that it shall not, by way of trade or otherwise, be lent, resold, hired out, or otherwise circulated, without the publisher's prior consent, in any form of binding or cover other than that in which it is published.

Contents

1. Moderately Dysfunctional Family — 1
2. Small Talk — 14
3. Resurrection of Affection — 29
4. Walk Cum Mock — 44
5. Play Way Manufacturing — 58
6. The Dress of Contention — 71
7. Storm Without Warning — 83
8. Tense Teens — 96
9. Sequential Troubles — 107
10. Show Show and More Show — 112
11. The Beauty and the Beautician — 118
12. Reaching Marryland — 126
13. The Nostalgia Club — 136
14. Men of Spirits — 143
15. Being a Hostess is No Joke — 151
16. Whiskey-Shiskey — 160
17. Make Room for the Groom — 166
18. Everyone Loves Gossip — 173
19. No Dearth of Freaks — 185
20. Will She Won't She — 190

1

Moderately Dysfunctional Family

Saturday 16th November 2019. No one has the faintest of ideas that a cunning virus is about to make a mockery of the human race in a few months.

The enterprising residents of Ludhiana, the industrial city, are allergic to frugal living and philosophical thinking—they aren't impressed by someone content with dal-roti-sabzi, khadi-wearing, who spends his evenings reading Kafka. In fact, the Ludhianvis live each day so grandly that a group of aliens could very likely hurl a big meteor at the city in a fit of jealousy. When Ludhianvis are praying for a boon, the word 'Mercedes' is a common part of the chant.

The Rahejas live in Elite Enclave, a locality every Ludhianvi aspires to have a bungalow in one day—complete with Deutschland-bred cars fuelled by a combination of fossil fuels and envy, patrolled by uniformed security guards who are miserly with smiles and liberal with salutes, and ringing with the unconditional love of pet dogs of hitherto unseen breeds who walk with their nose in the air.

Just before dawn, after the stray dogs have gone off to sleep having exhausted themselves after a night of noisy battles over zoru and zameen, mates and territory, the birds sing. The chirping of birds presents the illusion of being near a dense forest, populated by Mowgli and his animal friends. But the crows, mynas, pigeons and parrots of Ludhiana love the hustle and bustle of the city too much; they would suffer from clinical depression if sent away to a forest.

The Rahejas are a small family. The three generations live in above average harmony. Unlike many others in Ludhiana, the household is not lorded over by a patriarch—one who uses a judicious mix of affection and bullying to micromanage his family members—instead, there are multiple centres of power in the house, including the school-going Lakshya.

Reeti, the daughter of the house and the stunning beauty, is ever ready to loosen the family's purse strings and has been justifiably nicknamed as the C.E.O. (Chief Economic Offender) of the house by Kushal, her husband. She is the earliest to get up in this morning, with the aid of the modern-day rooster—the trusty alarm clock. Its tone is so jarring that one feels like throwing it away with enough force to hurl it towards interplanetary space.

The prospect of turning heads at a long-awaited wedding celebration that evening provides Reeti with enough thrust to escape the attraction of her king-sized bed. Her feet feel the cool Italian marble before she dives into her slippers.

As usual, Kushal is deeply slumbering because he was the last to doze off; not only in their house, but in the locality too.

Kushal takes credit for being the night watchman with a notional emolument—the ethereal calm of the night. Even the watchman coursing down the streets is often jealous of Kushal's affair with the night.

Reeti often tells Kushal, 'You live life like a tourist, as if it's a gala with minimal responsibility upon your shoulders. But I have to be on my toes all the time to care for all the eccentrics in this house!'

The full-throated alarm seems to be perceived by Kushal as the buzzing of a bee—he sleeps as if he is in a coma. Reeti's close friends, with whom she has a 'no secrets allowed' pact, often give her a 'no holds barred' description of their heavenly, early-morning lovemaking sessions with their spouses. But all Reeti can do is fantasize. The culprits responsible for this anomaly in her love life are Kushal's 'girlfriends'—books of various genres. He gets cosy with them after everyone else has dozed off, sleeps well after midnight and thus, remains oblivious to the worldly and the otherworldly charms of the dawn.

For Reeti, Kushal's bibliophilia is a total waste of time because his perusal of the covers haven't led to any tangible benefits. Kushal's industrial enterprise has been showing a growth rate even lower than that of the Indian economy before liberalization. What's more, he isn't even envious of those whose earnings per day exceed what he makes in a whole month. Rather, he is in awe of Sanket, the noted Delhi-based environmental lawyer and his old classmate. Sanket provides complimentary services to his esteemed clients: the rivers, lakes, air, birds, animals, trees and insects.

Reeti likes to gawk at Kushal when he is asleep. With his relaxed lips and cheeks, Kushal has a child-like innocence. She is also intrigued by his posture while sleeping—the foetal position. Reeti read an article in the *Women's Age* magazine, which suggested that such persons are insecure at a subconscious level. It corroborated what Reeti felt--he wasn't worldly-wise either.

'He might be worried about his pretty wife getting bored of him and falling for another man,' she feels. In fact, Reeti loves it when Kushal role-plays as a baby during lovemaking; it turns her on.

She can't help but plant a kiss on his cheek. But Kushal responds with only a minor twitch.

'Thank god he is not a woman,' she smiles. *'Or anyone could take advantage…'*

Only a month back, Kushal had tried to affect a new persona as the husband of a modern woman—a man ready to share all labour with his lady, except that of bearing a baby. He had gotten up early and enthusiastically begun a crash course in domestic chores under the skilled Reeti. But his innings in this avatar lasted only two days. He created so much upheaval in the kitchen that the orderly and clean Reeti had to do a quick re-think. *'If things continue this way, there is a distinct possibility of losing my mind… and that would be catastrophic for the family because there would be no one to maintain order!'*

In fact, Kushal had realized on the first day itself that he had grossly underestimated the complexity of home management as well as the unsung contribution of Reeti in their lives. Next day, in order to engineer a quick exit, he deliberately spilled some flour on the floor and let the milk over-boil. Predictably, Reeti declared the kitchen as a red zone for him.

Lakshay, their hyperkinetic seven-year-old son, too, declared that his papa's touch felt thorny to him and only his sweet mom had the privileges to get him ready for school. So, Kushal was back to his old ways: late to bed and late to rise, but without labelling it unwise. He had made some sharp observations about friends who followed the dictum of early to bed and early to rise—some weren't healthy, few weren't wealthy and most of them definitely weren't wise.

The God-fearing Reeti usually said a prayer before beginning her day, since it would be impossible for her to not act ungodly at least a few times during it. Images of Lord Shiva, as well as Guru Nanak Dev-ji, adorn the walls since the family is hybridized, religiously speaking. The whole world knows that Kushal is the odd man out as an atheist. Yet he has never tried to convince Reeti to be likewise; he feels that religion has a calming influence on her and he can't take the colossal risk of her straying into uncharted territory.

However, when Reeti asks him to accompany her for a pilgrimage to Maa Vaishno Devi temple or the Golden Temple, he refuses point-blank. 'A place has already been earmarked for me in hell and there is no scope for any change in my status! And there is a good possibility that I will have hardened criminals and scamsters for company!'

Reeti often prays, 'God, please pardon my husband for not paying obeisance to you. I try my best to compensate for him. He is mostly a good human being, though a bit more than what is required in the era of kalyug.'

Even as she descends the stairs abutting the high-ceilinged lobby to reach the kitchen on the ground floor, the house-proud Reeti looks for patches of dirt on the floor or particles of dust she may have missed in the nooks and corners. Luckily, she doesn't utilize the magnifying lens for this purpose, otherwise she would go nuts.

Kushal is not as innocuous as Reeti thinks him to be. Recently, he has reconnected with his ex—Diksha, a Delhiite, after eighteen years, courtesy Facebook—the friendship factory. For the last few days, they have been chatting on WhatsApp and also calling up each other, the explicitness increasing in graphic progression. Right now, Kushal is having the dream of dreams. He and Diksha are as physically close as two creatures of the opposite sex can be, while Somesh, her husband, is away on business. Their carnal trip is in full swing. Suddenly, Somesh appears in front of them with a Prem Chopra-esque expression. Pointing a revolver at them, he says, 'I was suspecting this for quite some time. I got a duplicate key made for the bedroom and cut my trip short. Now both of you can continue your affair in hell!'

Kushal jumps to shield Diksha in a flash, and raising his closed fist, he points it right at Somesh.

'You loser! You don't have it in you to fire a weapon,' he bellows.

Somesh closes his eyes and presses the trigger; Kushal wakes with a jerk. His heart is pounding like a mridangam at the climactic end of a classical recital.

He rubs his eyes. *'Was this dream a sort of warning? Anyway, now that I have woken so early, I should surprise my wife number one!'*

To counter the inertia of rest, he gets up from the bed with a swift jump. Then, he tiptoes towards the kitchen.

Reeti is at the counter, stirring a pot.

'Good morning, meri jaan,' he says, with 'feeling'.

Reeti turns around and lets out a mocking squeal, 'Bhoot! Bachao!'

Both of them share a good laugh.

'How is it that you have woken up without me having to beat you into shape?' she teases.

Kushal decides to try his hand at something he has rarely done before—putting on an act. 'I had a dream so bad that it was able to shatter my sleep, which, you know, is unrivalled for its intensity.'

'Did you witness an apocalypse?'

'Sort of. It was an environmental disaster. The city was engulfed by such a thick smog that I started to feel breathless. You rushed me to the hospital without even a smidge of lipstick! But no bed was available since hundreds of patients had already reached first. In between gasps, I told you to take good care of the kids in my absence, and to not hesitate to marry again! Just when I was about to go into cardiac arrest, I woke up,' Kushal says in a rush.

'That is…really strange. Most married men dream of their ex-girlfriends or secret girlfriends! But I have no issues with your dreams about air, water and earth!'

'I admit, I am a crazy environmentalist. But…the thing I care about the most is the immediate environment. Here, I always find a stunning lady with hazel eyes,' Kushal says. Then, he drowns in her eyes before giving her a quick peck on her forehead.

Reeti folds her arms. 'Statutory warning—Diverting attention in the kitchen can cause mishaps.'

As she speaks, she is reminded of the milk boiling in the saucepan. Reeti rushes to switch off the burner. 'See? That was close.' However, she has savoured an early morning kiss from Kushal, which is as rare as the flowering of bamboos.

Kushal has always had a way with words. 'Speaking of diverting attention, when you walk along the road in *that* jeans and *that* top, you too create a dangerous situation! Distracting the occupants of the vehicles! They're probably asking God what crime they have committed to not deserve a wife like you!'

'Shut up, Kushal. Don't talk so cheaply,' Reeti scolds. Kushal notices the difference between what she says and how she feels— Reeti wears a faint smile. Obviously, her endorphins are flaring after Kushal's flattery.

'You married a cheapster!' Kushal laughs as he retraces his way back to the bedroom.

He remembers the lines from the song, *'Live to Tell'* by Madonna. 'A man can tell a thousand lies, I have learned my lesson well,' he hums. '*I can compete with Natwar Lal*,' he mutters to himself.

He lies down to complete his quota of sleep, and returns to his dreams of Diksha.

Soon, Reeti's fingers are propelled towards an object that is necessary for a model citizen of Ludhiana—the iphone.

Most of her WhatsApp groups are loaded with 'good morning' messages, otherwise leading to a tremble across servers and the internet cables. Reeti is not convinced by the quotation she reads in one of the posts; it exhorts one to shun materialism and survive just on spiritual wealth. She knows that at the first sign of her becoming an ascetic, her friends are going to boycott her and label her as a 'gone case'. She is also aware of the fact that those who forward such posts chase nothing but money, use it to buy Hidesign handbags and piggyback on it to initiate or cement relationships.

Then she comes across a post wishing everyone a perfect day. She doesn't get carried away by this either. There are many in her vicinity to ensure that this would not happen: her lazy maid, eccentric father-in-law, hyperkinetic son, foxy mother-in-law and impractical husband. Even if all of them decide to behave on a particular day, social media would make sure to give her a jolt from at least one of these disasters:

- Her name fails to appear on the guest list for a happening party.
- She doesn't get zillion likes and comments on a photograph she has posted.
- Her friends announce a new arrival—a brand-new luxury car.
- She finds pictures of friends and relatives holidaying in places she can only dream about.

Reeti opens up 'Tip Top Girls', her core WhatsApp group. They are tip-top without an iota of doubt. But the word 'girls' is a misnomer because all of them are married, on the wrong side of thirty and forty, battling with the fine lines appearing over their faces, conspiring to have them classified as aunties. It is next to impossible to enter this group—these women love erecting a lofty barrier which social climbers find too hard to surmount. The intellectual types are also not welcome since they wear dresses that the Tip Top Girls won't even attempt to wear at funerals.

Reeti has a lament. She does not like missing out on the WhatsApp group where the ladies seem to have the most fun. This is known as the 'Naughty Girls' group, and justifiably so, because any not-raunchy post is declared taboo in it. But she has opted out of this group because of Lakshya, the little brat. If she joins it, someday or the other she is likely to forget to delete the raunchy posts. If Lakshya happens to catch a glimpse, he might show the posts to her father-in-law or mother-in-law and announce, 'Look, Mom looks at dirty pictures!' She has tried to keep a password on the phone but Lakshya invariably forces her to reveal it to him. He has learnt the fine art of getting his way—initially, he entreats, then he whines and if these don't work, he can even go to the extent of rolling on the ground.

But all this social media content isn't just a way to waste time. In Reeti's circle too, there are quite a few entrepreneurs who peddle products like cakes, sweets, couture, jewellery, handbags and cosmetics, as well as services like make up—the kinds of things which increases by the day. In fact, one lady has already begun to fish for a customer, so early in the morning, and has put up a handbag for sale. Reeti is contemplating a similar venture of her own; banknotes earned by her would feel crisper, she believes. It is not too difficult to find customers here—often the sales are made on a give-and-take basis and the use of coercion and emotional blackmail isn't frowned upon.

Leaving aside Instagram and Facebook for later, Reeti starts to get ready—she loves this part of the day because her mirror showers her with liberal compliments. Reeti scans her face from above, then downwards. She has arched eyebrows, big hazel eyes, high cheekbones, full lips, sharp nose and an oval face; what more could she ask for? A faint smile creases her lips—most of her beauty is God-gifted, but there has been some contribution from sculptors in white coats.

Reeti applies make-up and finishes up styling her hair too; she is helpless against the impulse to take a selfie, an impulse which can besiege her even during slow mornings. Also, the sparkling stainless-steel utensils in the kitchen double up as mirrors and she can't cut a sorry figure in front of something so shiny.

Back in the kitchen, Reeti has fired up all the four burners of the cooking gas stove to prepare multiple dishes since everyone in the house is a fussy eater. In this respect, they are like children. For every meal, she is expected to take the family members on a national and sometimes, an international culinary tour. In fact, if she cooks routine stuff for a few days at a stretch, Kimti Lal, her father-in-law, makes a face or even says, 'We are eating dal-roti-subzi too often. Forget about what my doctor says. I prefer *quality of life* to longevity!'

Three days ago, Reeti had seen a video on Facebook about the dangers of using one's mobile phone in the kitchen, and it even involved an actual fire. But after having abstained for two days and suffering incapacitating withdrawal symptoms, she decided that the risk-reward ratio was in favour of using the mobile. She also took solace from the fact that there were people more reckless than her, such as people who smoked despite the images of smokers with terminal stage lung cancer on the packets.

Reeti now prepares Lakshya's school tiffin by herself, just as she used to for her daughter, Vanya, who now was at boarding school. *'Love imbues the food with extra nutrition. My poor Vanya. She must be missing my heavenly food and motherly touch.'*

Drops of tears form in the corner of her eyes but they are not heavy enough to flow down her cheeks.

Reeti does appreciate what she feels is among the few good qualities of the Rahejas—they don't have a culture of bed tea. The folks at her parents' home are the opposite; everyone makes a long face if denied tea in bed first thing in the morning. However, the Rahejas are big fans of milk and its offspring, like curd, paneer, khoya and butter. The family has a variant of obsessive-compulsive disorder common in Ludhiana: milk many times a day. However, Lakshya has been so overfed with dairy that a lone glass of white milk has begun to look like a glass of liquid phenyl. But Reeti, like every other Punjabi mother, fears that an inadequate amount of milk consumption will lead to her child becoming a weakling and that there would be consequences for it at a later stage—she will be turned away from the gates of heaven for being a lousy mother. So the milk is given an attractive makeover, and Lakshya happily laps up varieties of milkshakes, unless he is in the mood to bug Reeti. In such a case, the scene switches to a *Tom and Jerry* cartoon—Reeti following Lakshya around with a tall milkshake glass in her hand while he dodges her by swiftly jumping over and around tables and sofas.

Tripta, Reeti's mother-in-law, even washes her face with milk, though it hasn't been able to halt the long march of wrinkles. Had milk been more affordable, she would even have taken baths doused in it. Long back, the family even had a buffalo in the house, but that phase ended when the municipal corporation ordained that all dairy cattle must live outside the city limits; after all, the four-legged creatures had reduced the speed of four-wheelers to that of a bullock cart. Reeti is aware that Kushal too knows how to milk a buffalo—although he hasn't mastered the more important skill of milking customers and suppliers of the auto parts industry.

The word 'milky' is used while describing the skin colour of the family members. In fact, Kushal is the only one in the family with a 'wheatish complexion' and it is because of this that he has been subjected to overt and covert racism. His siblings and cousins often jest that he doesn't look like a part of the family. When Kushal was a small kid, he was told by his elder brother that he looked darker than him because he had been found as an abandoned infant inside a rubbish dump and had subsequently been adopted. He had believed this story for a long time and suffered many insecurities and tribulations as a result.

2

Small Talk

Early mornings are also the best time for Reeti to call up Jasmine, her mom, because she can chat to her heart's content; there is a little chance of anyone eavesdropping. In any case, their conversations are quite predictable.

They are unlikely to touch upon the following topics:

Greta Thunberg

String theory

Climate-tipping point

Judicial backlog

Craig Venter

Postmodernism

Using earphones, Reeti keeps her hands free to carry on with the chores, which also include futile visits to the maid's room to wake her up.

Kushal knows of this daily ritual. He had taunted Reeti a few days ago, saying, 'It seems like you are still attached to your mom by the umbilical cord.'

Pat came Reeti's reply. 'Sort of. But it is beneficial for you too. Guess how?'

'No idea,' he had replied; scratching his head for a full minute had failed to yield an answer.

'Since I am able to vent stress about my day-to-day problems to my mom, I fight less often with you—only as much as is required to spice up our love!'

'I guess I also figure prominently in these "day to day problems"?'

'Absolutely! Living with a freak is easier said than done!' Reeti had said and Kushal had accepted defeat in this friendly war of words.

'Hi, meri sohni baby. How are you?' Jasmine says, her voice reeking of love as pure as spring water from the highest reaches of the Himalayas.

'My dear, my super Mom, I am good. I can't wait to attend the event hosted by the Kumars tonight. To tell you the truth, I have been planning to attend this marriage for months now. I want to be the shining star of the party!' Reeti says with a twinkle in her eyes.

Narinder Kumar, the father of the bride and Reeti's cousin, owns two woollen mills apart from other disclosed and undisclosed assets. But he has been feeling the pinch over the last few years—global warming is threatening to shrink the winter season as well as his profits. He dreams of an ice-age so severe that even the population of Kerala and Tamil Nadu need to wear *his* products to survive. Narinder has a peculiar hobby—he gets a different Bollywood diva to endorse his brand every new season, without taking economics into consideration. For his daughter's marriage too, the initially planned budget has been exceeded by a wide margin. He remains unruffled in the knowledge that he can always sell off a plot of land—he is rumoured to have quite a few in every locality of the city. Even birthday parties of his family members reveal an expenditure that have left jaws agape.

'Are you going to tell me what you are wearing today? Or do you want to keep it a secret and reveal it at the venue?' Jasmine asks.

'I will tell you, Mom. But on the condition that you keep it to yourself! It is a totally new concept which will make the others down vote the couture houses where they get their dresses from! My one-piece is a mauve coloured fusion dress. It features embroidery in the front but the cut is modern—a lot of my back, shoulders and legs are going to be visible. But I am not ignoring my face; I have booked a makeover session at the best salon in town. Today, I won't mind if the men stare at me, I think even the decent ones wouldn't be able to help it!' Reeti giggles, her hands dancing like that of an enthused Ted-X speaker.

'I know, my darling daughter is always in style. After all, you have my genes!'

'True! So what time are you reaching the venue. Obviously, I will have to add one hour to whatever time you tell me…'

'Actually, I will have to waste my precious time by reaching the venue on the dot! I have an invitation from the family of the bride as well as the groom.'

'Great!'

'There is nothing great about it! I will have to give shagun amount to both sides!' Jasmine chuckles. 'During this month, the shagun-giving for different celebrations has left me poorer by forty thousand rupees. And much more has been spent on dresses and jewellery, which as you know, have been exclusively made for every occasion.'

'Ma, did you attend the engagement ceremony of Dad's cousin's sister-in-law's niece?'

Jasmine frowns. 'Yes, dear. But they belittled me by gifting me a cheap salwar suit. I think they got it as a present from somewhere else and just dumped it on me. Anyway, I will pass it on to someone else!'

'I told you—that family has no standards! If you are not going to do it in style, why celebrate at all? They behave as if all of their money will be transferred to a bank account in heaven! See, I enjoy my life to the fullest. And that too despite having a husband who is just so-so at making money.'

'I know, beta. I can understand your situation.'

The pressure cooker whistles and interrupts their conversation, but only for a long second.

'Most of the industrialists in Ludhiana change cars every year or so. But we have had the same Mercedes for the last five years. This gives me an inferiority complex,' Reeti says in a low whisper.

Jasmine is afraid that her darling daughter may start to cry. So she emphasizes that the glass is half full and not half empty. 'You should take comfort from the fact that he is faithful to you, which compensates for his poor business acumen. Remember, there a flip side to marrying men who are very rich and very handsome—either they chase girls or the girls throw themselves at him!'

'Kushal doesn't stand a chance even if he *tries* to fool around. He is addressed as uncle by ladies in their thirties and forties, and he looks like one. So I am safe.'

'I, too, have noticed that whenever the both of you are seen together in a picture, he looks as if he is your uncle, father or whatever. Why doesn't he get a hair transplant and maybe some procedures for tightening the skin? Men can nowadays be finicky about their looks. They will soon start applying make-up too!'

'I have suggested that he visit a cosmetic surgeon. But he replied, "I don't care about my appearance anymore because after bagging you I have nothing more left to achieve." Ma, you know very well that I have won all the awards at kitty parties and local beauty contests—Mrs Ludhiana, Mrs Beautiful Smile, style icon and many others—but the title for the most stylish couple has always eluded us! Kushal seems to take my loyalty for granted. Sometimes I think I too should have a rich and handsome boyfriend! So many men make passes at me and some of them are much younger too. A woman dating and even marrying a younger man is not a rarity anymore!'

'Shut up. You are crossing all limits. Don't try to ape western culture so blindly. In our society, all sorts of extramarital affairs are taboo, and this includes emotional attachment with another man. You have had enough flings before your marriage! Never ever say this again,' Jasmine says in a saccharine voice, concealing her surprise.

'Oh, mom. It was just a joke! If I had to go astray I would have done so by now.'

'All right. I am hanging up now. Otherwise, the maid will skip cleaning some of these rooms,' Jasmine says.

Reeti gives her mother all the credit for her own happy, married life. Just before Reeti's marriage, Jasmine shared with her the tips and tricks so Kushal would continue to dote on her as he used to during their courtship.

When their first child was about to be born, Kushal wanted the delivery to be performed by the trusted grey-haired family gynaecologist, Dr Surkiran, who had delivered him too. However, Reeti argued that the hospital where Dr Surkiran worked was housed within an old building and she would suffer an irreversible loss of status when her friends and relatives visited her after the delivery. Also, her kid could suffer from chronic depression later in life once the child discovered that the birth took place in a drab looking hospital. So they decided on going to PJ Hospital, a plush corporate hospital, and opted for the costliest private room.

After Vanya, her daughter, was born, Reeti was advised by her mom to take a break from childbearing—'for at least three years'. But the couple found out the hard way that babies couldn't be summoned from heaven at will; the combination of Kushal's virility and Reeti's fertility failed to click. Reeti knocked at the doors of deities, prostrated herself at the feet of babas and allowed herself to be financially exploited by astrologers and fortune tellers of all hues. But, throughout, Kushal remained steadfast in his conviction that they could only be helped by those humans in white aprons, men and women who could create miracles with their treatments based on evidence-heavy research.

'Even if you pray, stand on one leg or walk barefoot for ten kilometres to visit a religious place, it is not going to work,' he had said to her.

'Oh God! Please forgive my adharmi husband for his utterances and always shower your benevolence upon my family,' she had prayed immediately.

Ultimately, Lakshya, their son, was conceived by IVF. However, Reeti insists that her repeated prayers catalysed the miracle. She also attributes Lakshya's restless nature to the assumption that something went wrong in the test tube.

Since her parents live nearby, Reeti often visits them and also takes Lakshya, the prank factory, along with her. Her parents dote on her, although she has always been a bit of a rebel, partaking in ground-breaking acts in the family—wearing short skirts, drinking, dating boys openly and having a love marriage. They did try to rein her in but succeeded only in bits and patches.

Kushal makes full use of her absence from the house by watching documentaries on streaming services for hours together, and asking Reeti to join him is the same as offering her juice of the bitter gourd. She loves only those shows which induce emotional highs and moist eyes.

On the rare occasions that Reeti and Kushal have a nasty fight, she threatens to leave for her parents' home and to stay there for good. But it is less of a threat and more of a bargain.

At such a moment, Kushal folds his hands, 'Please don't leave me. I have lost the skills to live without you.' Reeti melts like an ice candy under the hot sun and hugs him.

Sona, the maid, finally enters the kitchen after spending more time than Reeti does to get ready.

'The maharani has arrived,' Reeti mumbles. She can't dare to annoy her by waking her up before 7 a.m. Reeti has to turn a blind eye to many other shortcomings although Sona too keeps her cool when Reeti goes into phases of unwarranted umbrage. *'Even if a new maid is employed, she is not likely to be any better. Ah, the sincerity and affection of Ramu Kaka from old Hindi movies is extinct. But neither do we have employers who seek the help of Ramu Kaka to counsel their rebellious son or daughter!'*

Reeti is well aware of the ground reality: her friends who haven't been able to find a maid for quite some time feel like wretched creatures. In fact, she has started avoiding some of them because whenever she comes across them, they pester her with their pleas. 'Please get me a maid, Reeti,' they parrot.

'Namaste, bhabhi,' Sona says and takes over the kitchen, like a relay runner taking the baton from her. She is wearing branded jeans with a trendy top, which Reeti herself bought her a few days ago; maids are rarely exploited in Ludhiana, and it is mostly the other way round now. On that very shopping trip, Sona coaxed Reeti to buy stuff for her siblings too and Reeti gave in without even a token resistance.

A television has been installed in Sona's room so that she can regularly shed tears while watching dramas to prevent the accumulation of toxic thoughts in her mind. Sona has picked up some undesirable traits from Reeti's family too—like a certain fussiness about food. Her taste buds are at loggerheads with the aloo paratha, porridge and egg bhurji, which are on the menu for breakfast today.

'Bhabhi, can I make poha for myself?' she asks Reeti; Reeti assumes it is just for the sake of asking. Reeti is being pampered with one of Sona's daily doses of respect since Sona knows she will get her way anyway.

'Sona, you are becoming so choosy day by day. How will you manage when you go to your in-law's home?' Reeti says with a wink.

Sona blushes and chooses to keep mum.

While Sona is walking around, Reeti can't help but stare at her and covet her curves. But she takes consolation in the fact that once upon a time, she too could describe herself in terms of inches. However, during her pregnancies, Reeti was under tremendous pressure to give birth to a 'healthy' child, which basically implied a new-born weighing more than 3.5 kg, one who would make everyone beam with pride, including the gynaecologist who delivered it. For once, her mother and mother-in-law were in agreement: she had to be force fed lots of pinnis and panjeeri, laced with pure desi ghee; even a heavyweight wrestler would have developed a paunch after eating all that stuff. Whenever Reeti protested about 'over-nutrition', she was told that she could skip the time-tested recipes at the risk of having a baby who would be nicknamed sukdu (shrivelled), tilli (as thin as a matchstick) or lakeer (a thin line); she would be a mother who had left her child to suffer being a misfit in

Ludhiana society, where physicality and prosperity complement each other. The weight gain took even longer to shed than the duration of her pregnancy despite tough posturing by the gym instructors.

Although Reeti is still a regular gym-goer, she is not able to wear a two-piece bikini, during vacations on beaches, comfortably.

There is a saying in Ludhiana: 'Once your expenses and tummy are enhanced, they can never be reduced to their original level.'

Reeti enters the room of her in-laws. Kimti Lal, her father-in-law, is asleep. During winter, he goes into semi-hibernation and often skips the morning walk.

Reeti bows to Tripta, her mother-in-law, but stops just short of touching her feet; Tripta, too, raises her hand in the blessing pose, while maintaining a respectable distance from the hair on Reeti's head. Tripta seems to have come to terms with her countless wrinkles and folds, which have happened due to years of co-ordinated efforts by the gravity and laxity of her skin. But she never lets even a single grey hair show—her weekly hair dye application is never missed.

'Both of us seem to be afraid of catching some sort of infection from each other,' Reeti muses to herself.

Reeti and Tripta mostly use their grey matter—and sparingly, their vocal cords—to gain an upper hand over the other. This creates a façade of harmony within the house. Often, the maids and other domestic help are made pawns in their power games, but they too add fuel to the fire by setting them up against each other, enjoying the twists and turns of saas-bahu serials live.

Kushal has stopped meddling or mediating in their bilateral issues because whatever stand he takes is construed as nepotism. In fact, whenever he goes abroad, he brings home identical gifts for them both, or else his jet-lag may be exacerbated by two dissatisfied ladies, both with the same accusation: discrimination. Tripta feels that she is at a disadvantage vis-a-vis Reeti because Kushal still seems to be as infatuated with Reeti as he was when he had brought her home as a young bride.

Mother and daughter sit on the sofa, which has now found a place in the bedroom after being evicted from the main lobby—a younger generation of sofas have usurped it there.

Tripta asks Reeti, 'Beta, what time are we leaving for the marriage celebration tonight?'

'Hopefully around 8 p.m. Usually I make everyone late but today I will set a new record in punctuality!'

Tripta lifts her chin. 'I am sick of seeing Kushal wear the same clothes for as long as I can remember. They are not even fit to be used as wipes! You must hold him by the scruff of his neck, take him to the market and buy him some fashionable stuff.'

'Mummy ji, mostly he listens to me...but when it comes to dressing up, he acts like an obstinate donkey! According to his weird philosophy, to save the world, we should consume as little as possible.'

Tripta's frown lines deepen even further. She hasn't liked the use of the word 'donkey'. She performs a silent and careful analysis and is finally able to discern that Reeti hasn't called her son a donkey but has only compared a habit of his to the donkey's.

Tripta continues nonplussed, 'Kushal is still under the influence of his old friends from JNU. These guys live in a world of their own. No wonder many of them are still driving small cars and living in rented flats! I still rue the day my husband and I agreed to let him go to Delhi to study journalism instead of sending him abroad for an MBA.'

'If he refuses to accompany me to the market, I will buy apparel for him and tell someone to gift it to him. In addition, I will, quietly, burn a few of his vintage clothes by ironing them at high temperature!' Reeti smiles, glad that she and Tripta are connecting, even if it means making fun of her beloved.

Next, it is time for Reeti to wake Lakshya up. Today, he is asleep in his room, though he usually prefers to sleep next to his grandparents. But Reeti and Kushal don't seem to mind this for they can get more creative (and even noisy) while making love. Whenever Lakshya is asked the reason for preferring the geriatrics, he says with a naughty smile, 'My papa snores very loudly.'

Actually, before he sleeps, Lakshya likes to listen to the stories his grandma narrates; she brings them alive with dialogues, gestures and facial acrobatics. However, all he receives from his mom and dad are sterile renditions from story books.

Lakshya is indeed a cute child. His hazel eyes take after his mom while the dimpled chin is inherited from his dad. His chubby cheeks, which acquire a rosy tint in winter, make him irresistible to ladies, young and old, who can't help but kiss him. But Lakshya is also naughty, possessing skills like the monkey's climbing and hopping, and the interiors of the home have had to be done up in such a way no fragile and artistic object is within his reach. However, Reeti still manages to impress the guests who visit their home by saying, 'Our interior designer planned such a minimalist décor because this is the in-thing in Milan now.'

Lakshya's vaccination and paediatrics check-up are due in a few days. But Reeti has already decided to send him with Kushal. Even the paediatrician folds his hands as soon as Lakshya enters his chamber. Initially, the little brat scans the room for any sweet-looking child to tease. If he doesn't find one, he looks at the office table for any interesting object, something worthy of exploration and then picks it up without caring to receive the doctor's permission. Persuading him to get examined is a project in itself. When he finally lies on the table, he acts so ticklish that even the touch of the stethoscope on his chest makes him giggle.

Reeti says, in honey-tinged tone, 'Lakshya, mera sohna bacha, please get up.'

But Lakshya only turns to his side.

Reeti continues, 'Come on. You are a good baby.'

'No, I am a bad boy,' Lakshya says, waking up with an impish grin. His quick wit could put an adult to shame.

As usual, he gets up only when Reeti sets aside her decency. 'Your school bus is likely to leave without you. Then, you will be marked absent and taken to task by the principal.'

Rameeta Sharma, the principal of Lakshya's school, is one of the few who can admonish Lakshya, making him transform from Mickey Mouse to a meek mouse.

Reeti has to keep an eye on Lakshya while he is taking a bath. If left on his own, he often splashes water all over the bathroom to make it appear like he has taken bath.

Then, it is time for breakfast. Lakshya is aware that until his stomach is filled, Reeti feels emptiness in her life.

'Today I have made very tasty aloo paratha for you. Do you want it with butter, curd, pickle or tomato ketchup?' Reeti asks.

Lakshya bobs his head sideways. 'Mom, I want to have custard today. We ate potato curry yesterday. Everyday aloo, aloo, aloo!'

'So, your preferences keep changing every moment, like a one-time password,' Reeti mumbles as she sets out to fulfil the demand of this modern-day prince.

There is still some time before the school bus is to arrive. Since Lakshya has been denied a personal mobile phone, he borrows Tripta's phone. Reeti tries to peep over his shoulder when she finds him typing a message on it.

'Bad manners, Mom!' he says and quickly deletes all the messages he has recently sent.

Respecting mobile handsets is a recent milestone for Lakshya to have achieved. For quite some time, everyone in the family had had to buy only the most basic smartphones because a number of high-end phones had suffered an early demise through Lakshya; Kushal had even nicknamed him, 'the serial killer of mobile-phones'. Some were drowned in the bathtub or flushed down the cistern, while others succumbed to a fall from the first floor. His curiosity killed another handset when he dismantled it to take a look at its insides.

After making him climb the steps into the school bus, Reeti orders, 'Don't pull on the braids of another girl today, okay?' For Reeti and Kushal, meeting the parents of the kids who have been harassed by Lakshya, with folded hands, apology-ready on their lips, has become a routine. Paradoxically, this has also triggered friendship with some of the parents of Lakshya's classmates.

Reeti doesn't get worked up over Lakshya's mischief unless he tries to ape the action of his favourite superhero and risks getting hurt. She follows the dictum—running an industrial enterprise requires a person who is prepared to bend or break a few rules when needed, someone who is adept at dealing with people, ranging from the saintly to the ghastly. In fact, Lakshya has been firmly instructed by Reeti to not be friends with the son of a teacher-cum-social worker who resides in their neighbourhood, to keep him from developing a character like that of Shashi Kapoor in *Deewar*.

Even Lakshya's grandparents don't want him to grow up into a copy of his father. They rue the day when Kushal, who was a teenager at that time, had been sent during summer vacations to stay at the home of Tripta's brother, who had a library at home. Kushal picked up the habit of reading there and since then, he has been physically present in Ludhiana, but mentally, he is residing in Utopiana.

3

Resurrection of Affection

For his daily dose of physical activity, Kushal prefers the walk around the park in the morning to the sweat of the gym. He finds added value here–chatting with his gang of 'morning walk' friends, all of whom are jolly and most are roly poly. They don't mind having a three-roll belly instead of a six-pack abdomen because they have many other things to flaunt. Although his friends often poke fun at him for his unorthodox viewpoints, Kushal takes it sportingly; he knows he is the odd man out in Ludhiana.

Skipping the gym also helps Kushal avoid the gym instructors, those typical men with their Type A personalities who set steep targets and make a fussy eater like him consume the most despicable foods. And if he fails in this, which he is certain to, he would be made ashamed of his rudimentary willpower.

Since the park is some distance from his home, lot of walking happens just to reach there. But this has a flip side too. Sometimes, the acquaintances he meets on the way turns out to be an excessively social animal. He is then entreated to enter their home for a cup of tea along with its ideal accompaniment—a chat. That day he mainly walks down memory lane.

Kushal steps out of the gate of his home. There is a little nip in the mid-November air, but it is nothing compared to mornings of late December and January, when the cold seeps in right up to one's bones. He looks at the trees along the boundary of his house and whispers to them, 'Sorry, my friends.'

These majestic creatures, they have been condemned to live as dwarfs. He wants to see them in their full form, hosting lots of birds, insects and squirrels, vexing the ladies of the house with a litter of fallen leaves. But everyone else in the house gangs up against him on this issue–as if it is a question of *their* life and death. Reeti, Tripta and Kimti have a fixed idea—if the front elevation of the house is obscured by trees, high society will turn its back on them. So the gardener mercilessly prunes the trees, and Reeti shows him some mercy.

In fact, Kushal sees that the whole lane is bereft of tall trees. In the newer construction zones, the landscape designers, keeping in mind the sensibilities or rather, insensibilities, of their clients, get only shrubs or small trees planted.

Kushal has also been barred by his family members from installing large capacity solar panels on the rooftop; he has been given the explanation that they would shine, blinding visitors at the front of the house and make it seem like they all lived in a house belonging to a mad scientist.

He walks, passing the adjoining house where the curved balconies are being demolished by the exterminators—the labourers—who specialize in reducing structure to rubble. For the last few days, their hammers have brought on headaches in the vicinity, but nobody is complaining. In Ludhiana, remodelling one's home is an activity more respectable than worship and social service.

Gulshan, their immediate neighbour, is getting the exterior of his house re-modelled for the third time in a decade. Whenever a new style of exteriors comes into vogue, he seems to be attacked by an intractable itch; only the alteration of his house can relieve it. If Kushal had his way, he would have called the local, and even the national media, to draw attention to this madness. But how can he go against a person who would come to his aid even if he called him past midnight? Even if Gulshan is not likely to be of much help because he finishes his last drink only half an hour before midnight. And if he bumps into Kushal late in the evening, Gulshan flashes him a smile, which is as genuine as homemade desi ghee. 'Come on. Let us have a few drinks and some gup shup.'

Whenever Kushal has accepted the invitation, he has clinked glasses with Gulshan at his home, to the accompaniment of chicken tikka ordered from the iconic, 'Chache Da Dhaba—since 1934'. Often, their impromptu party carries on for too long and Kushal receives a missed call on his mobile phone from Reeti, which he interprets in this manner—'enough is enough, come home, or I will be forced to use words I usually keep in reserve.'

Usually, at such a moment, Gulshan promptly says to Kushal, 'Have one peg more. Reeti is going to shout at you anyway.'

A black mask is hung in front of Gulshan's house to ward off the evil eye.

The rationalist in Kushal rises up in protest and he grimaces at the mask. *'The chic exterior is being constructed to generate envy. So many evil eyes are going to be directed at their house anyway.'*

The extra-large frame of Gulshan suddenly appears in front of him. He has just returned from his pseudo morning walk, completed after making two rounds of the park at a pace which has allowed even octogenarians to overtake him.

'Hi, buddy,' Kushal says to Gulshan with a mischievous smile. 'Two years ago, you had told me—and in a sober state—that you were firmly resolved that you would not touch this house for at least ten years. What happened? Have the curved balconies caused vertigo?'.

Even as Gulshan is conversing with Kushal, he keeps on gazing affectionately towards the house. 'You guessed right, Kushal. I have been feeling suffocated for quite some time because of the out-dated exteriors of my house. See, some people sell cars in prime condition just because they have taken a fancy to a newly launched model, others use up their valuable bank balance in holiday trips abroad. But I have simple vices. I want to renovate my humble abode and drink within limits set by me! Also, new year resolutions are not the only ones which are meant to be broken!'

'All the best,' Kushal says, knowing very well that even God would need to employ strong arm tactics to stop Gulshan from having his way.

'Thank you for your warm wishes. Enjoy the late morning

walk!' Gulshan says and walks into his new home.

Kushal's early morning dream of Diksha has been a profound experience. He is still reeling from the effect. All things now have the power of suggestion to bring back memories of Diksha—a pretty lady passing by or even a butterfly of the same shade as her favourite colour, yellow. He reminisces.

A few months after joining the journalism course at the Jawaharlal Nehru University in New Delhi, Kushal came under the influence of Saurabh, his neighbour, who in turn was a follower of Greenpeace. He was indoctrinated, much as a soldier would be, and his sole purpose in life was to defend mother earth.

One of Kushal's write-ups, and it had been widely circulated, read as follows:

> These bloody humans! They are hell bent on destroying this amazing planet. And instead of asking citizens to live a life in tune with nature, governments are encouraging them to consume more and more. That is how the so-called modern economy works, that is how the coffers of the government are being filled. In the near future, rampant pollution, nuclear war or an epidemic by a super bug will lead to the extinction of the so-called master species, which is actually the exterminator species, because it has led to the eviction of millions of other species from the face of the earth. After tens of thousands of years, the monkeys will again evolve into humans who will discover our fossils and label us as hominids. But these humans too will commit the same mistakes as us. The vicious circle will go on and on and on...

Kushal and his classmate Diksha, a Delhiite, connected because her train of thought was as off-centre as his own. As a bonus, she was attractive. Unlike girls from Ludhiana, Diksha didn't take a multi-staged entrance test to allow him some space in her heart. Soon, they were an inseparable couple who seemed destined to travel together till their sunset years. In the mornings, they explored the vast sea of knowledge within their university campus; in the evenings, they explored the lesser-known historical monuments of the city; at night, they explored the others' anatomy. Diksha was such a good kisser that he often wished that their foreplay would never end. He also loved the way she used to cling to him when she rode pillion on his bike; she loved it when he called it an attempt to murder him by stopping his breathing.

After finishing his degree in journalism, Kushal joined the *Aaj Ki Taaza Khabar*—a newspaper that tried hard to live up to its reputation as the 'quickest to get news', even if it meant making its reporters drive like a maniac or sending them right at the focal point of a riot. Here, apart from a boss with a perennial scowl, he had to contend with a bunch of foxy colleagues who had mastered the liberal art of snatching credit from the newbies.

Presuming that an employer couldn't get worse than this, Kushal tried his luck in another newspaper. Here, the boss didn't have fits of rage but he expected the greenhorns to slog without even glancing at the clock and to remain mum about employee rights.

Once, Kushal came in the way of a stone hurled by a violent mob; but that didn't deter him and the wound healed quickly.

The idealistic young journalist toiled day and night to collect a story, something with the potential to effect a mini revolution in his country. But the story was thrown in the dustbin by the editor, ostensibly under the influence of an influential person. Kushal now had first-hand experience of the flip side of the sunlight when he suffered sunstroke on a field assignment. Prompt hospitalization helped him escape becoming a martyr to the journalistic cause.

Finally, Kushal decided to abandon his experimentation with truth, untruth and pseudo-truth. There was no choice but to return to the city he had always considered unsuitable for 'his type'. He also tried to bring back a souvenir in the form of Diksha. However, Diksha was firm in her view that smart girls migrated to smarter and bigger cities and not the other way round. For this, she was even ready to tolerate severe heartache.

During their last meeting in Lodhi Garden, Diksha had looked at him with a mask-like face. 'I am sorry for hurting you but the fact is that I don't have feelings for you anymore. Just think of me as a dream and never try to contact me again.'

When Kushal got up from the bench to leave, he looked into her eyes. They were sitting in a secluded corner of the garden and a parting kiss would have been a balm to his wound. But she lowered her eyes and he walked away—without looking back.

Kushal shifted back home. But he was hoping against hope. *'Diksha still loves me. Thoughts of me are going to torment her so much that she will be forced to board the Shatabdi express to Ludhiana.'*

But in vain; she upheld the reputation painstakingly built by women through the ages—their behaviour cannot be predicted by applying any algorithm, logic or even, intuition. She blocked his phone numbers and consigned all his mails and messages to the trash folder. Finally, it dawned upon Kushal that he and Diksha had made another addition to the long list of ultra-short-term love affairs, the stellar contribution of the twenty first century to new social mores.

As is common with many youngsters, he blamed his parents for his weakness and his failure to ascend in his career. *'My mom spoiled me by pandering to all my demands, including the grossly unjustified ones! And Dad went one step further. When I was eighteen, he got me a car when I hadn't even demanded one.'*

Some of Kushal's industrialist friends, with offspring who are currently studying for professional degrees in metro cities, are worried that the kids will develop greater affection for their adopted cities and that they won't visit Ludhiana, not unless they feel like having puri sabzi from Babey Di Hatti. In that case, the industrialists cry, their dream of retiring from their family enterprise will always remain a pipe dream.

But Kushal allays their fear by elaborating on the 'Kushal's Hypothesis', which is simple—'Leave your kids to their own devices. These spoilt brats won't last more than a season in their jobs. Just like me! They will come back to Ludhiana and will entreat you to let them into the family business. When that happens, you should act a bit pricey; take some time to agree to their request!'

Having returned to Ludhiana, Kushal decided to follow the

dictum, 'one should follow one's passion' and set up a bookstore for general books. But he soon learnt that sayings aren't absolute truths. Actually, if he'd conducted a market research, he would have realized that most Ludhianvis use books as paperweights. The timing was also not right; mobile phones and social media had started to colonize all circles of life. Even the kiosk selling chana bhaturas, right opposite his store, fared much better than him. The book store wound up in a few months, much to the delight of his father who welcomed him into the family enterprise with open arms.

Soon after, an incident occurred, and it right away cleared the air and showed the attitude of the general public towards literature.

He went to a book launch along with a like-minded friend. Just when they were about to enter, a clean-shaven kurta clad man with disorderly grey hair, who seemed to be an impassioned writer, asked him in a stern voice, 'Yes, please. How can I help you?'

'We have come to attend the book launch,' Kushal said, surprised by the demeanour of the man; why was he behaving as if they were trying to trespass into a secret nuclear facility?

Then, the author did an about turn. He sported a wide grin. 'Oh! I thought the two of you had lost your way! Usually, the audience consists of poets and writers only, all of whom know each other. Please come in.'

After they been seated, he addressed the crowd, 'See we have genuine audience here today.'

All of them stood up and clapped. Kushal and his friend

were seated in the front row, on the sofa, as guests of honour.

Kushal joined the automobile parts industry, which was run as a family enterprise. He had the most important qualification to be appointed—straightaway in a senior position—fifty percent of his father's genes. His dad assigned Kushal the job of tackling the foreign clients. This was apt since Kushal was unlikely to have a blank look on his face, even if the foreign client deviated from talk of business and started querying about the origin of yoga or the crux of Vedanta philosophy.

Just a few months after kicking Kushal out of her life, Diksha understood why romantic love had been given such an exalted status in folklore. Thoughts of Kushal were peskier than calls from telemarketers. Guilt about having acted stony-hearted and denying him the parting kiss had also set in. She devised a solution—to marry as soon as possible. This would make her move on, get over Kushal. Also, it would mend her relationship with her parents whom she had been vexing for a long time by acting autonomously, even when their advice had mattered.

But, as it often happens with tasks done in a hurry, there were complications.

Somesh, her husband, was from a filthy rich business family. However, during their honeymoon in Paris, Diksha noticed that whenever she tried to strike up a conversation about art, culture or the cuisine of France, he looked like a student who had just read an out of syllabus question in an exam. After they returned to Delhi, a jealous relative spilled the beans. Somesh hadn't even passed his matriculation; he was a graduate on paper courtesy of fake degrees. It was now clear to Diksha why all intellectual talk was French to him. His smile was genuine though and he doted on her. After two kids were born in quick succession, Diksha's expanding universe did an about turn—it condensed to the home and the family.

For a long time, Kushal and Diksha were content with secretly checking each other's Facebook profile page or sneaking a peep into each other's life through common friends. Then, Diksha suffered a sudden, massive 'heart' attack and the only way for her to survive was to send Kushal a friend request on Facebook. When Kushal read it, he clicked the confirm button within milliseconds. They got to talking. Nostalgic scenes of good times spent together were recreated vividly as both of them developed selective amnesia about their ugly break-up.

After walking a bit, Kushal reaches the house of his turbaned friend, Karamjit Singh Grewal. Through the open gate, he spots the six-foot Karamjit leering at his BMW 7 series car, almost like he has just kissed it. The designer plate at the back of his car reads 'Brightonian' in bold letters, conveying that Karamjit has become blue-blooded after having studied in the Bright Student School at Dehradun. It also exhorts those who have not studied in a boarding school in the hills to make amends by getting their kids into such a school. The nameplate has 007 as the last digits. Obviously, James Bond is his idol, although he has never had the equivalent of 'bond girls' in his life—his wife is his first and probably, the last love. '007' has been purchased from the transport department for an amount with which one could buy yet another small car.

If anyone asks Karamjit what he does for a living, he replies—I am vehla (idler). In truth, he has his hands full with the upkeep of his numerous rural and urban properties spread all over the Punjab. After purchasing a house in Surrey, British Columbia, the mini-Punjab of Canada, he has even become an international landlord.

'Hey, what's up? You seem to be in love with this car!' Kushal chuckles.

Karamjit's face flushes. 'The car is my second love. It is way behind my wife.'

'I think it's the other way round. You are just making a diplomatic statement! But jokes apart, this is an extraordinary car,' Kushal says.

He knows the best way to connect with Karamjit is to appreciate his car; it would be inappropriate to praise his pretty wife who is just two inches shorter than Karamjit in her socks and taller than him when she is wearing high heels. Kushal also knows, from experience, that in Ludhiana, putting a scratch on someone's car is equivalent to teasing his wife or girlfriend and the reaction is proportionate to the political and muscle power of the car owner.

Karamjit's face lights up as he says, 'On the G.T. Road, this beauty feels so stable—even at a speed of 140.'

Kushal has seen Karamjit's posts on social media. He has been posting pictures of the speedometer of his car with readings much higher than that. He makes a mental note to feign sickness if Karamjit offers him a ride in his car to go out of station. *'Drivers like him reinforce the Indian habit of praying before embarking on any journey on the highway, and making offerings after reaching the destination in one piece.'*

But to cheer his friend, he says, 'Wow! That's great!'

'Only five BMWs with similar configuration exist in Ludhiana city,' Karamjit gloats.

'But you are an even rarer specimen!' Kushal says with a wry smile and gets on with his walk.

'That was a good one liner!' Karamjit says to Kushal's retreating form.

Kushal can't help but think about his favourite car—his eyes had moistened when it was resold long back. The steel grey Maruti Zen had played the role of a 'middleman' in cementing Kushal and Reeti's bond during their courtship days. They had a phase where they would go on long drives while listening to *'I Will Always Love You'* and other lovey-dovey songs, but it was brief. Soon, they sought secluded streets with non-functional street lights. Kisses and cuddles yielded to higher degree of intimacy under the able direction of their primal instincts. Despite being extra watchful, they often had close shaves with watchmen, policemen and voyeuristic men. It made it even more thrilling.

On the way to the park, Kushal comes across Billoo, the stray dog with catty eyes who lays claim to the street. The watchman of the locality has adopted him and calls him his son, his beta. He never barks—unless another stray dog tries to trespass on his territory, and then he turns into Sher Khan. Billoo doesn't harass the pet dogs—he is pragmatic enough not to mess with those who are well connected.

Kushal pines to bring a canine into his home; he could have an obedient and loving family member whose only demands would be cuddling and eating tasty grub. Also, the number of visitors to their home are likely to be reduced since dog phobia is quite common in Ludhiana. But Reeti has already refused with a firm 'no' to his proposal because her mom has announced, 'I won't even set foot in your house if you keep a pet dog.'

Kushal never fails to smile when he reaches this vacant plot of land, otherwise owned by Shurli, his friend. Shurli has a heart of gold but also has a penchant for providing unsolicited advice. His friends appreciate his caring nature, but that hasn't stopped them from giving him a nickname: 'mummy'. The plot has a volleyball court, along with a room to which a kitchenette is attached.

A year ago, a few 'out of shape' men of the colony decided that they could get over their guilt of eating puri channa every Sunday morning at the shop of Manga Halwai by playing volleyball later on in the day. One day, a mischievous dark cloud interrupted their game and made them take shelter in the verandah. Shurli suggested that the onset of monsoon needed to be celebrated with beer and as expected, everyone cheered. Since then, ending the game on a high note, with beers became a ritual. One fine day, they decided to skip their volleyball game and had an exclusive beer drinking session. Soon, the volleyball club became history. A beer belly started to protrude from Kushal's light frame. Two months ago, Reeti warned him that if his belt size kept increasing, she would leave him for someone else. Although Reeti didn't actually mean it, the word 'someone else' hit him like a blow to his balls and he left the group immediately.

The next block has imposing bungalows with tall boundary walls; most people in Ludhiana look upon these properties as the Mount Everest of their aspirations. But Kushal sees these big houses as Godzillas, with their huge appetites for the earth's precious resources. He is also allergic to the water guzzling grass lawns and wishes that his favourite living beings, the trees, would usurp such spaces.

Whenever Reeti is fresh from visiting one of these houses on a social call, she blurts out multiple superlatives about them in one go. This vexes Kushal because she is obviously implying that the interiors of *their* house, which had been done up just three years ago, are in the pre-historic category and need to be changed. She also makes it a point to estimate the total worth of these mansions and then conveys the figures to Kushal, indirectly hinting at his inability to earn mega bucks (though he is contented and unmoved). Kushal feels that Reeti is unlikely to ever develop dementia because she is constantly exercising her grey matter over money matters.

The gate of the home of the Goyals is open; the driver is parking a car inside. He notices a Jaguar, which is obviously their latest toy. They already have two Mercs, an Audi and a BMW.

Kushal is more amused than impressed. *'What if someone visits their house in a Bentley. Will the family need the services of a psychiatrist for their collective depression?'*

4

Walk Cum Mock

Packs of stray dogs roam the park. But they recognise Kushal as a harmless regular and look at him with disinterest. He is not worth even a bark. Kushal enters the well-maintained park and sets his right foot on the footpath. There are only a few walkers, talkers and joggers. Peak morning walk hour has ended because the early risers have already left after finishing their walk, and are currently in varying stages of readiness for their adventurous foray into an urban jungle. Within the next moment, he is overtaken by a lissome lass.

His mouth is half-open.

'What is this—could be a supermodel—doing here? She seems to be a newcomer but she will surely enhance the prestige of the colony even more than the industrialists here.'

Moving quickly with long strides, she is soon out of his sight—but not out of his mind. An old man is practicing his yoga, but instead of activating the inner eye, he seems to be keeping an eye on the walkers. A group of old ladies, each of whom is a bulky manual of practical wisdom and surveillance skills, are sitting on the benches after a symbolic walk. They are lamenting about the deteriorating willpower of the young brigade to rein in their needless needs and expanding expenditures.

Finally, Kushal spots Jagat, a member of his 'Late Morning Walkers' gang. Jagat's upper eyelids, which are normally droopy, have dropped further, and his eyes are small slits. The rest of the face appears dismal too. It is as if all the whisky bottles in his well-stocked home bar have been transformed into apple juice overnight.

'What happened, Jagat? The last time I found you so down was when your ex refused to acknowledge you at a party,' Kushal inquires.

Jagat gives his friend a forced smile. 'Prince, my son, is trying to assert his independence, but a bit too prematurely. Yesterday, he went to a movie with his friends without caring to inform the family honcho! When he came back, I scolded him in vintage style, to remind him that parental control hasn't gone out of fashion.

But he simply replied, "Chill, Dad. What's the big deal?" He then went on to inform me that his schoolmates, which includes boys as well as girls, smoke, drink and a few notable ones even take hard drugs. Then he announced that he stays within certain boundaries—limiting movie-watching to one film per week, playing video games for only a few hours at a stretch, eating a pizza without the cheese burst option—he actually meant that he was doing me a favour by being only a minor deviant instead of a major one!'

'How times have changed,' Kushal lamented with him. 'When I was a kid, my dad and the physical education teacher of my school seemed to be competing with each other to whack me the hardest.'

Jagat takes a good look at Kushal. 'Today your face seems to be aglow…as if you have found a new love.'

Kushal's hair rises. *'Wow! This guy is so observant. No wonder the turnover of his industry is always going north.'*

'Yaar, this glow is because of a moisturizer—which I stole from my wife's cupboard! You know very well that I am inseparable from Reeti and otherwise also, I am a man of principles,' Kushal says with the panache of a seasoned actor.

They begin to walk together at a slow pace. Kushal keeps an eye on the surrounding trees and shrubs for any interesting sights. Soon he spots the common jay, a striking butterfly with blue wings, sitting on a hibiscus shrub. He tells Jagat, 'Look at that beauty. I am going to take a picture on my phone, wait.'

Jagat stops for a moment and then resumes walking. 'I will join you at the same place after a round of the park,' he says. Kushal has tried his best to interest his friends into nature-watching but has had a zero-conversion rate. Still he hasn't given up all hope.

By the time Jagat comes back, Kushal is still chasing the restless butterfly. It has not yet given him an opportunity for a good shot.

Jagat holds him by his arm. 'Come on. Let's go.'

Kushal has no choice but to go with the flow.

Chaman, another member of the gang, joins them.

'Bookworm, how are you doing?' he addresses Kushal.

Kushal smiles, *'I am willing to take any number of taunts in the name of my beloved, my books.'*

'I am doing okay, but I am often stressed because I have gotten myself embroiled in multiple responsibilities—my difficult-to-please family members, the tough-to-manage industrial enterprise and difficult-to-protect affairs of the natural world,' he replies profoundly. *'Add to that a clandestine affair,'* he mutters to himself.

The baby-faced Chaman is the joker of their pack. In fact, whenever he attends even a funeral in the family, a few relatives have to keep constant watch over him; on a few occasions, he has even gone to the extent of satirizing the deceased. But he is demanded at parties because he manages to amuse even the most unhumorous persons with mocking of self, his wife and some incorrigibly insincere relatives. Chaman leads a balanced life—he gulps down five large pegs of whisky every evening and tries to balance this by walking five kilometres in the morning. There are many more in Ludhiana who follow variations on the same theme.

'How are things at your end?' Kushal asks Chaman.

'Bekaar! Yesterday I got poorer by twenty thousand because of my wife,' Chaman says. 'If anyone else lost such a huge amount of hard-earned money—or even ill-gotten money—he would have lost the ability to smile for at least a few days.'

'Did someone snatch her handbag? Every other day there is a news item about snatchings in the city,' Kushal asks.

'No. A handbag snatched money from her!'

'What?'

'While surfing the net for online shopping, she chanced upon an offer wherein a handbag was being offered at twenty thousand rupees, after a supposed discount of seventy percent. To make the offer even more irresistible, it was mentioned that only a few pieces were left. Sarla went into a trance and paid the amount by credit card. But soon after, she realized that she had been conned; it was a fake seller. Modern thugs don't need to mug their victims. The computer keyboard is far more effective,' Chaman elaborates.

'Did you shout at her? It's a rare opportunity that has come your way!' Kushal says with an impish grin.

'There was no remorse on her part, which is why I am so upset. Rather, she defended herself by arguing that a sale of seventy percent could have fooled anyone. Also, it was her first offence in this category!'

'Deals and offers are my enemy too. Reeti just can't resist them. She falls into the same trap over and over again. If it is written in front of the showroom that the sale will end in a few days, she reads it as if it is saying that if you don't buy from us, the world will end in a few days. And if she reads that there is a sale on the sale, the showroom becomes a black hole for her; she is sucked into it immediately,' Kushal reveals.

Chaman is relieved to know that he is not alone. 'Our wives don't realize that a garment showroom is not a charitable organization that doles out cheap clothing to make the world a better place.'

The tall hot girl overtakes them. All of them smile at each other.

Chaman is the first to speak. 'She is married, with a young child, and her husband is a lawyer.'

'Unbelievable. She looks newly-married and that too around the minimum legal age. The moral of the story is that if you have a disciplined lifestyle, anything is possible,' Kushal says.

'What is discipline? The last time I heard this word was when I was in school,' Chaman laughs.

After they have walked a few metres, Jagat says, 'What were we talking about? After seeing that lady I have become disoriented!'

'Jagat, if I ever want to rob you, I will simply set up a honey trap,' Chaman says, and all of them get their recommended daily allowance of laughter.

Soon, Kushal returns to his sob story. 'Sharp minds behind the fashion industry ensure that a number of dresses become redundant every season; even medicines have a longer expiry date! Nowadays there are shops and even websites to rent party clothes. But, Reeti thinks she will catch some sort of infection from these outfits, even if they have been dry-cleaned. In fact, we have run out of space for her dresses and her footwear, and we have already purchased extra almirahs. I often tell Reeti that I might need to hire a warehouse for her.'

Chaman adds, 'And I have told my wife that if her dresses are joined from end to end, the length will be equivalent to the earth's distance from the moon!'

Kushal feels a blood rush to his head. 'I think all fashion designers should be told to shift to alternative professions and wearing unfashionable clothes should be made compulsory for all citizens.'

'If that actually happens,' Chaman says in a low voice, 'my garment factory would also have to close down.'

Kushal comes to his senses, realizing that realism easily decimates idealism when one's own survival is at stake.

The trio have already taken six rounds of the park, one more than they usually do, but the conversation is so spicy that they want to carry on.

Jagat also senses an opportunity to unburden himself. 'I have an even bigger enemy: the ladies' kitty parties. My wife attends no less than eight in a month. This includes an outdoor kitty, also known as the Kasauli kitty. The ladies leave for Kasauli in the morning, treat their lungs to some pine-scented air and then have a lunch party. By evening, they come back to Ludhiana—for some more socialising! If I tell Sheena to cut down on kitty parties, she gives me this explanation. "If I try to leave any group, all members come to meet me as a delegation and threaten to go on a fast unto death unless I reconsider."'

Chaman laughs, then attacks from a different angle. 'You guys are running down the ladies without listing your own excesses.'

'I agree. There is no need for us to imbibe Single Malt Scotch whisky if we are going to gulp it as if it were country liquor,' Kushal chips in.

'I change my car every year because it is my hobby. So I blow up as much money in one sweep as my wife spends over a year,' Chaman agrees.

'My farmhouse is neither being used as a farm nor as a house,' Jagat confesses.

'Farmhouses are meant for misuse—not for use!' Chaman says with a crooked smile.

'This is precisely why I don't handover its keys to you!'

Chaman continues, 'It is not a man's world anymore. The ladies don't take things lying down. Shrom, one of my cousins, was caught red-handed by his wife. She was tipped off about his dalliances with his girlfriend in the guise of farming at his farmhouse. He pleaded to be given one last chance but his wife *actually* left him. And now there is a complicated divorce case going on.'

Kushal's legs start to quiver. *'I hope I don't meet the same fate as Chaman's cousin. There is still time. I can always cancel the trip to Delhi with some solid excuse.'*

But moments later, he steadies himself. *'I have planned it so well that my chances of being caught are almost nil.'*

Kushal and Diksha are almost a week away from their planned sentimental cum licentious reunion at New Delhi. Reeti's maternal family has a unique tradition. Once a year, Reeti, her parents, her sister and the kids, go on a holiday trip. During this phase of reinforcement of the sibling-bond, the presence of husbands is seen like a fish bone in a fish fillet. So, they have been told—in straight language—that they are not welcome to join this particular trip. But there is a consolation. During this period, the husbands are left alone and phone calls to them are infrequent. The trip is due in a week. To coincide with it, Kushal has already booked a train to Delhi and has informed Reeti about his so-called business trip. Diksha too has done all the groundwork.

When the group disperses, Kushal realizes that they have grossly exceeded their routine rounds, covering a long distance. As he is walking towards home, his body feels stiff. *'My vitality is decreasing and my virility will soon follow. Viagra use seems imminent. What if I don't perform well when I sleep with Diksha next week? I hope she will understand that at this age I can't be as good a performer as I was in my college days, back when she used to call me "horsy" and had even boasted about how long I lasted to her best friend.'*

After reaching home Kushal goes straight to the bedroom and collapses on his bed. He doesn't even have the energy to take off his shoes, but the fear of Reeti's out-of-proportion reaction to the offence makes him reconsider.

After half an hour, Reeti shakes him a bit roughly to wake him up—knowing that gentleness is unmistakably unsuitable for this unique task.

'Last call for passenger Kushal to board the flight to Timbuctoo!' she says, sounding like ground staff at an airport.

Kushal yawns and straightens up. 'No choice then. Must leave the couch of bliss,' he says and gets up with a jump. He kisses Reeti on the cheek; the lip lock is ruled out because Reeti has already applied lipstick and lipliner with the finesse of a make-up artist. But his kiss is adulterated—he is imagining that he is with Diksha.

For Kushal, getting ready is no big deal. He wears whatever clothes he finds, as quickly as he can find them in the almirah; his only concern being that the onlookers shouldn't mistake him for a beggar. Kushal spends less than a minute in front of the mirror. As a youngster, he thought of himself as average looking; presently, he doesn't even compare his appearance to other men. He has lost the demarcation between his forehead and scalp. Jowls, horizontal forehead lines and crow's feet are in their infancy, but have otherwise combined to effect the look of an 'experienced person'. Kushal has thought of growing a moustache to compensate for the lack of hair on his head, but whenever he talks about this to Reeti, she purses her lips. 'No means no!'

Then, Kushal moves downstairs towards the glass-topped dining table for breakfast. His salivary glands are feverishly pumping saliva into his mouth over the prospect of his taste buds having an encounter with aloo parathas laced with homemade butter. But Reeti is well prepared to counter the friendly onslaught of white butter.

She calmly places a single tablespoon of butter onto his plate. 'That is all you will get.'

Reeti has been coached by her friends that strictness of the wife has a direct correlation with the patency of the blood vessels of the husband's heart.

Kushal lodges a strong protest. 'Darling, this is like a jewellery showroom owner giving a measured quantity of precious metal to his artisan!'

Reeti straightens, her neck arched. 'If you had good self-control, I wouldn't have to do all this. Anyway, reach home in time this evening; you have to visit the venue to give a symbolic helping hand to my cousin. You might have to give him some advice—impractical or not—when it comes to making arrangements. You know very well that Narinder holds grudges for long. It is as if he notes them down in a diary! If he feels like you have ignored him today, he wouldn't cooperate when it is time for *our* daughter's marriage. We might even have to borrow some money from this filthy rich fellow.'

'But Vanya has already made up her mind,' Kushal argues, 'She thinks that *our great country*, the one that has given the world the zero, numerals, yoga and meditation, is not worth living in. Obviously, she presumes that Canada is a slice of heaven.'

This is a topic for which Reeti is always in the driver's seat. 'So what? Even if she settles abroad, I would prefer an Indian boy for her. Indians make better husbands than firangis. Although there is no scientific study to prove this, it is the general consensus among my friends and relatives settled abroad.'

'Ha ha. The lesser evil theory! I think it is just a myth. I wish that she finds a firangi boy by herself so that I am spared the inevitable financial emergency at the hands of the morbidly fat Punjabi wedding,' Kushal says with a crooked smile.

'How selfish. What are you earning for?'

'I was just joking,' Kushal says, relenting. He fears that any further discussion on this topic could turn Reeti into the modern version of the hunterwali.

Kushal has finished the allotted amount of butter with his first paratha. For the second one, he will have to make do with curd and pickle.

'Register this in your brain once and for all.' Reeti begins, 'I will not settle for less than five events for my Vanya, including a destination wedding!' Reeti now imagines insanely expensive dresses, venues lit up by a million lamps, a smattering of superlatives from the guests' mouths, and the jealousy-inducing social media posts.

'Done,' Kushal says. He looks as if he has just signed a surrender document.

'Okay, don't forget to bring the fancy envelopes from the Empress Gift Shop for putting in the shagun amount,' Reeti says, with special emphasis on the word 'fancy'.

The paratha isn't tasting as good to Kushal anymore. *'I can't believe this—the bundle of shagun envelopes I brought last month is already finished. The approximate money spent on shagun would have been enough for a trip to at least one of the "hundred places to see before you die".'*

'Why don't you get an envelope from the nearby stationary shop?' he tells Reeti.

'They are so drab!'

'The host will only appreciate the amount that has been put inside the envelope!'

'Just do as I have told you to. You don't have good taste in anything—except me!'

'Agreed,' Kushal says and walks away like a jackal who has been challenged by a tigress.

Although Kushal tries his best to live in the present, such talk makes him pay undue attention to the future. *'My ruin is as certain as the sunset. I will have to sell my spare property for Vanya's wedding. But Reeti, Mom and Dad will ensure that the budget is overshot markedly, forcing me to take a loan beyond my capacity.*

Soon, I will become a bank defaulter. The bank will take over my factory and I will have to go back to where I started from—as a newshound in Delhi. The alternative will be to commit suicide by drinking liquor continuously over many days. If I survive this phase somehow, I will have to work out arrangements for the silver jubilee celebrations of our own marriage anniversary. Reeti will insist on a re-enactment of our marriage, with dhoom dhaam. This will be followed by a month-long neo-honeymoon in Switzerland. That will again lead to life-long indebtedness. Even after I die, the creditors will harass me in the afterlife!'

Reeti reaches the gym, her number two addiction after selfies. Kushal is way down this list. Whenever Kushal plans a vacation, he makes sure that the hotel has a gym so that she gets to spend less time in the shopping arcade. Plus, he earns brownie points as a caring husband. There is also a hidden agenda—he sleeps like a log while she works out like a maniac during the mornings.

Reeti's friends and relatives often comment that she doesn't look like a mother of two kids. But, in the gym, there are a few damsels who make her feel grossly overweight, in accordance with the 'gym theory of relativity'. In turn, these girls wonder if they will ever look as chiselled as the cat-walkers seen on *Fashion TV*. This is good news for the gym owners. Contentment is a sure-fire exterminator of businesses and professions related to beauty and body shaping. Modern economists too are no fans of those who think like ascetics. They want every citizen to be a hedonist and with the help of credit.

But Reeti has a trump card. She beats all of them hollow

on bust size. *'Thank God, there is no effective exercise to develop big bosoms, and anyway, most women are afraid of breast implants.'*

Keeping in mind that every gram of melted fat matters to her, Reeti works out for some extra time, with an eye on the evening's celebration. However, her meditation session is taken over. Now there is little chance of calm descending over her mind, which is battered by a noisy barrage of thoughts about the storm she is going to cause in the evening. Later on, to maintain workout-life balance, Reeti and her friends get together at the gym café for some grub and plentiful gossip. The dishes, or rather the therapeutic delicacies, include antioxidant salads, immunity booster sandwiches and slimmer's burgers. The names are so impressive that just ordering them makes the ladies feel lighter. Reeti tries the newest addition to the menu: a sandwich called 'health is wealth'. But the chef has kept the café's wealth creation in mind too; he has made it so scrumptious that Reeti can't stop at one despite her best efforts.

For this session, she ends up with more calories assimilated than burnt.

5

Play Way Manufacturing

Kushal usually drives himself in his Maruti Ritz to reach his factory (although nobody in Ludhiana cares about the brand of a small car since it is equivalent in 'show' value to a two-wheeler). The chauffer-driven Mercedes is left at home, at the disposal of Reeti so that her daily commute in it keeps her levels of feel-good hormones at a high.

Recently, much to the amusement of his friends, Kushal had said at a party, 'I am the poorest Mercedes Benz owner in the city! But I have no choice, because if my family is sighted in a small car, our relatives would start a social media campaign to donate funds for us!'

The day the Merc goes to the service station, palpitations are guaranteed. When he goes to parties alone, he often skips the Merc and rides the Maruti Ritz—he is the sole industrialist in Ludhiana who dares to arrive to an event in a small car. If any acquaintance asks, 'Is everything okay?' Kushal smiles, 'I have fallen on bad days. But I wish no one else has to go through all this.'

As soon as he gets behind the wheel of the car, thoughts of Diksha return. It has only been a brief lull. He is surprised to feel a pleasurable sensation in his groin.

Before he knows it, he bangs into the rear of an SUV at the traffic signal. Luckily, he was driving at a slow speed. Kushal's immediate thought is, *'I hope the occupant of the SUV is not a typical hot-headed Ludhianvi.'*

A bearded giant comes out of the vehicle to inspect it. He has a good look at the rear end of his vehicle but can't find any major dent or damage. Then, he moves towards Kushal, looking unwaveringly at him. Kushal has noticed by now that it is the front bumper of *his* car which has suffered a crack.

Kushal says contritely, 'I am sorry. Just lost my concentration because some issue is occupying my mind. But I feel so relieved that neither of us suffered even a minor scratch. Thank you for your patience and cooperation.'

The man looks sideways. He is confused by Kushal's googly and decides to go back to his vehicle. *'It is good that he saw reason. If he had tried to hit me, he would have learnt a lesson—appearances are deceptive,'* Kushal mumbles after relaxing his right hand, which he had pre-emptively clenched into a fist.

'Diksha, you are a dangerous intoxication,' he mutters and starts practicing mindfulness, solely focusing on the traffic. Once the posh colonies give way to industrial zones of the city, more and more three wheelers are seen, including a few ramshackle ones spewing black fumes. The scene is reminiscent of the early industrial age. All moves to exterminate these outdated share autos have met a slow death.

Today, Kushal has forgotten his portable air quality monitor in a hurry. He knows by heart, the average PM 2.5 values at different locations for different seasons, having undertaken numerous observations over the past year, at the risk of blackening his lungs.

'Too much knowledge also has its drawbacks,' he often says. Sometimes, after finding high PM 2.5 levels at a particular location, Kushal begins to feel a constriction in his chest. But he knows this is just a functional symptom: pollution acts slowly and stealthily.

A man, with a handlebar moustache and a designer beard, whizzes past his car on a Royal Enfield Bullet motorcycle and then zig-zags to cross other vehicles, as if he has received a special pack of unlimited fortune from God. The rider is sans a helmet since hiding his face would defeat the whole purpose of riding a Bullet. The silencer of the motorcycle has been disabled to coax people to look towards it and the rider, and also to terrorise the motorcycles of inferior status.

'It seems, for him, a Bullet is even more prestigious than a Merc,' Kushal feels.

Next, Kushal encounters a speed-breaker in the form of a bullock cart transporting its goods. The driver of the cart doesn't seem perturbed by impatient motorists, seeming to say—'hit me if you can, I don't have much to lose'. Even the bulls moving the carts seem to take similar liberties and the blaring horns are but background music for them.

At a major intersection, the zebra crossing is overrun by vehicles. After all, many drivers view it as road decor. A specialist beggar, who seeks alms only on Saturdays, knocks on the side window of Kushal's car.

Kushal winds down the side window. He upturns his nose and pouts his lower lip. 'Go away. I am not afraid of God.'

The beggar's mouth opens a bit and remains in that position for quite some time. *'Although I have come across a few atheists, none has been as brazen as this fellow. If everyone becomes a non-believer, I will starve,'* he thinks as he closes his mouth.

'Let God be benevolent to those who give alms and also to those who don't,' he says and then moves towards another car.

Then, Kushal encounters a traffic jam—the aftermath of a minor collision. It has proceeded as expected. Instead of reaching a compromise, the drivers of the car have summoned their friends for practical exposure in hand-to-hand combat. Since both groups are well connected, the police are avoiding the use of force and are making a show of Gandhigiri to broker peace.

Kushal smiles. *'Judging by the crowd of onlookers gathered during these peak hours, it seems there are a sizeable number of idlers in the city!'*

At the next red light, where he has to wait a while because of congestion, Kushal passes time via people watching. A newly married woman is sitting pillion on a motorcycle, clutching her husband's waist tighter than is necessary to maintain her balance. Kushal can't take his eyes off the bright red bangles covering her lovely forearm.

The lady catches him in the act and looks him in the eye, making Kushal turn his face away. *'Oh God, things are going from bad to worse in this city. Even scholarly looking men have turned into oglers.'*

'*That was an over-reaction!*' Kushal feels.

Even before the signal turns green, the driver of the vehicle behind him honks incessantly. Kushal looks in the rear-view mirror. He shouts an expletive, which is heard only by him. It is the first of the many he will blurt out before he can reach his factory. The culprit, the driver of the mini truck loaded with milk containers, is trying to deliver milk—as fresh as possible, even at the cost of spilling blood.

Just after he has crossed the intersection, Kushal's eardrums are rattled by a pressure horn. He looks in the rear-view mirror. As expected, it is a private bus. There is no space to move, certainly no space to his left, but the bus driver again honks as if conveying that the lack of space is his problem alone.

These bus drivers are taught a special type of driving for the lanes: they drive in a single lane while others are made to change lanes, as if they are avoiding the path of a tornado. At the first opening, Kushal moves the car to his left and lets the bus pass. The bus almost brushes against his car. Another expletive helps him equilibrate his brain.

Soon, he finds himself behind a truck with steel rods protruding from its rear. With a red cloth tied at the end, the trucker warns him to come close only at the risk of being bayoneted.

Finally, he reaches his factory, situated in Focal Point, the industrial hub of Ludhiana. The watchman gives him a vigorous salute—although Kushal has told him so many times that he doesn't require ego-boosters.

Kushal has his priorities right. For him, nature is the greatest factory, which showers bounty without any expectation of profit and without causing any pollution. In fact, he has an earnest desire to sell all his assets, including the factory, and to use the capital to purchase a big parcel of land and plant a forest. He believes that if a number of capitalists combine towards this noble mission, even capitalism could be redeemed. However, he is afraid even to mention this to Reeti for she might label him a mad man, and do something drastic in a fit of her own homegrown madness.

He directly heads to the butterfly garden where a variety of flowering plants have been planted to bribe the butterflies with nectar. The lantana bush reveals a Great Orange Tip butterfly, which is captured on his mobile camera. The photograph is instantly dispatched to the WhatsApp group of Ludhiana Nature Lovers Club—a group whose members can be counted on Kushal's fingertips.

He enters his sprawling office, which has an attached room with furniture for different grades of relaxation: a sofa, a recliner and a bed. Even at the factory, Kushal maintains work-life balance, with slight tilt towards the latter—he reads books, titillates his taste buds by having food delivered and socializes through phone calls. All this is possible because he has an efficient manager in Sarjit Singh, to whom he has delegated—or rather washed his hands off—many of his responsibilities. Luckily for him, Sarjit is intending to continue in this manner; in Ludhiana, the drive to 'do your own thing' is so high that many managers set up their own ventures, often overtake their former employers and then boast about it to all and sundry.

Just after they were married, Reeti had expressed the desire to take up an active managerial role in the factory. However, Kushal had dissuaded her at the time since the factory was doing well and he didn't want to disrupt the status quo. A year ago, Kushal had felt that he now needed Reeti's help in the factory. But this time, Reeti refused, explaining that she had gotten used to an easy life; in any case, her schedule of parties, shopping and taking care of the home and family left her with hardly any spare time.

In the room, Kushal gets on with routine practices, which include meetings with the managers and the supervisors. He calls them 'very innovative' because they come up with a new set of problems every day. Some of these issues are easily solvable, while others make him feel like leaving everything and settling down in an ashram within a secluded valley in the mountains. The accountant rattles him further with the information that some of the accounts are in a tangled mess and a longish meeting with him would be needed to sort them out.

After the strenuous workout of his brain, it is time to relax it with the aid of his smartphone. Soon, Kushal finds the masala he had been looking for: a fight on Facebook. After a post criticizing the government was trolled by loyalists, it has become free for all. In the heat of the moment, netizens are using words like 'screw you' and 'bastard' with impunity.

'This is still better than rioting in the streets,' Kushal thinks.

Then, he opens up his WhatsApp. He has to check it frequently because if he misses Reeti's message for more than an hour, she follows it up with a phone call. If his phone is busy, she hears the automated reply: *the person you are trying to call is talking to someone else.* The phrase 'someone else' is equivalent to stinging nettle for her.

To his utter surprise, there is no WhatsApp message from Reeti; an event as rare as a total solar eclipse.

'She seems to be preoccupied with the preparations for the evening party; must be tense, like a student about to appear for their IIT entrance!' he smiles.

Then, there is a new message on WhatsApp and it makes him feel like breaking into a Bhangra dance. Diksha has painted his WhatsApp red by sending him a bouquet of red roses, red hearts and kisses from her red lips. For the last few weeks, Kushal has been revealing the deepest recesses of his mind to her and vice versa. Since Diksha has been occupied for the last few days, they have had to do with texting, which has recently acquired shades of pornographic quality.

Kushal tells Inder, his personal assistant, 'I am going to have a prolonged discussion with a prospective foreign client. Don't disturb me for at least half an hour.'

He calls Diksha as per their schedules.

'Hi, sweetie. What's up?'

'Hi, jaan, I am totally free.' Diksha coos. 'Also, there is no one at home. Today we can talk to our heart's content.'

'How is your new job?' Kushal asks.

'I'm enjoying it, although the salary is peanuts. But you, you must be printing money with the help of the machines in your factory.'

'Not exactly. Just enough for roti-kapda-makaan and an outdated Mercedes.'

'What happened to the journalist "with balls" who wanted to expose the men in power with "no balls"?' Diksha says and her muffled laughter is heard even before he can answer.

'Haha. Now I am taking advantage of the system! Balls to idealism!' Kushal says, making Diksha break into raucous laughter.

After a while, Diksha says, 'So, what are you doing for the weekend?'

'Attending the marriage celebration hosted by the famous Kumars. They are trying to overshadow all the previous marriages held in the city!'

'Listen, the time we spend talking is increasing daily, but it is still not enough for me. I think I am in love again. I remain on a high and I think of you all the time. We broke up in haste… it is probable that the flame of our love was never extinguished completely.'

'True. My condition is more or less the same. But there is a nagging thought. What we are doing is basically a sin. We are taking advantage of the trust of our partners.'

'Arrey yaar! Stop this morality business!' Diksha scolds. 'We aren't saints. And even among the saints, only a few are actually able to control their urges on a long-term basis. Also, have we investigated our spouses? They could also be connecting with an old flame—or a new find!' Diksha's voice is firm.

'I don't know. But you are right. Let us stop being self-critical. I feel like taking you in my arms. Right now!'

'Me too. Hey, let us do it on the phone. Something is better than nothing!' Diksha says coyly.

'Okay, let me think.'

After a while, Kushal begins in a husky tone. 'For the last few days, I have been imagining how we would make love when I meet you in Delhi. But right now, just visualize that both of us have found a chance to spend a night together, after a long hiatus, in a cottage at a mountain resort in the Lahaul Valley of Himachal Pradesh. It is very cold outside but we are smouldering with desire.'

'Yes. You are so hungry for me that you embrace me—so tightly—as soon as we bolt the door. But I tell you to wait and do it with style!'

'I nod in agreement. We sip red wine to inflame our passions even further.'

'I am in a burgundy-coloured negligee, the colour of which matches that of the wine,' she adds.

'We sweet talk for a while and then I slide my hand over your silky thighs. You close your eyes.'

Both of them pepper their conversation with sighs and moans. Soon, Diksha tells Kushal that she is discarding her clothes. They carry on. Just when their virtual act is near the climax, Kushal feels his mobile vibrate. He finds Reeti's number flashing on the screen. But, at this juncture, he can't let Diksha down. He moans loudly. 'Ahhhhh...I am through, darling.'

A wry smile passes over his lips. *'Thank God. Although men can't fake an orgasm in the actual act, they can do so over a phone call.'*

In a minute or so, Diksha has become silent, a sign that she too has reached the pinnacle of ecstasy.

'Okay, sweetie, I will hang up now. I am getting a phone call,' Kushal says with an air of urgency.

'It must be your sexy wife! Tell her that you were talking to an important international client who gives you a lot of business.'

'That is exactly how I was planning to hoodwink Reeti!'

'Hopefully, this will be in live-action soon! Bye, dearest Kushu!'

'Bye, Diku. Love you loads.'

Before he can dial Reeti's number, Kushal receives her call. Kushal's heart is galloping but it doesn't show in his voice. 'Hey, I just saw your missed call.'

As expected, the amateur detective queries, 'With whom were you talking to for so long?'

'I was trying to finalize a new deal with an international client.'

'I thought it was one of your girlfriends!'

For a moment, Kushal feels benumbed. *'Has Reeti inserted some spying app in my mobile?'* He steadies himself and manages to say, 'Good joke! You know very well that women are not attracted to an unsmart, ageing, married man.'

'No need for your explanations! There is only a remote chance of you going off-course, but it is there! I can't afford to lower my guard at any stage. Anyway, I rang you up just to remind you to come home in time.'

'Done,' Kushal replies.

He realizes this was a surveillance call from Reeti. She

had already reminded him in the morning to be back on time. However, Reeti's call has sent him on a bender of introspection. To this day, Kushal remembers the words he had said to Reeti when he proposed to her: 'I shall remain faithful to you till my last breath.' He had actually meant it.

'What if an extremely pretty damsel crosses your path?' she had said with a quizzical smile.

'Of course, I will have a cursory glance at her! But that's it,' Kushal had replied.

The couple have no discord of significance. They are both reconciled to each other's idiosyncrasies, which they have in plenty. By making sure that every meal she cooks or gets cooked is to his liking, she tries to keep the way to his heart permanently patent. They are in perfect symphony when making love. Reeti doesn't believe in acting coy in bed and isn't even afraid of telling Kushal whenever she craves lovemaking.

However, Reeti keeps on dropping subtle hints about him not earning enough and abhors his unorthodox agendas, like environmental activism. On the other hand, Diksha is a fan of his cerebral output and never judges him on the money front. Also, Diksha was the one who took the initiative to connect with him. There is a saying in Ludhiana—'If a man rebuffs advances from a woman, he will be born as a eunuch in his next birth.' For long, he has been listening to boasts of sexual prowess from his friends. He finally has a story of his own, although he plans to keep it to himself.

To get over his guilt, Kushal's thoughts move on into a different orbit. *'Is it possible that I am in love with both of them.*

Everywhere it is mentioned that one can love only a single person of the opposite sex at a time. Maybe virile men like me have a different brain biochemistry!'

After a while his phone pings again. His pupils get dilated after seeing Diksha's number flashing on the screen.

'You must be wondering if I have gone crazy,' she begins. 'That is true, I am! In a hurry, you forgot to kiss me goodbye. Also, few minutes ago, I had a brainwave. I can catch the afternoon Shatabdi train to Ludhiana and enter the marriage function in a party dress without arousing anyone's suspicion. I have already come to know about the venue of the marriage using my detective skills on Instagram. We could find some dark spot there and rediscover how our lips tasted!' she says, her voice oozing raw passion.

Kushal's mind seesaws between titillation and fright. But he ends up saying, 'Please Diku. This plan has a lot of pitfalls. We are meeting after a week.'

'Okay. I will try my best to control my impulses...but I can't promise anything. You might be in for a surprise!'

Both of them blow kisses on the phone and then hang up.

Then, it is time for necessary evil—work at the factory.

6

The Dress of Contention

At home, Tripta has just become free. Her 'rummy club' friends have left after a rush on 'pure sequence'. She pays attention to Kimti who, by now, has read each and every line of the newspaper, except for the matrimonial columns.

'Anything special in newspaper today?' Tripta asks like an inquisitive child.

Kimti looks at her. He gets respect from her in quanta, and that, too infrequently.

'In a country as big as India, a lot happens on a daily basis. However, all of that can't make it to the headlines. No newspaper will ever mention that a lady named Tripta is taking very good care of her good-for-nothing husband! But I did find an article that gladdened me. Roshni, the celebrity dietician, has written that we can consume desi ghee in moderation,' Kimti replies.

Tripta's face brightens. 'That is good news. Both of us should re-introduce it in our diet.'

'But Reeti is a fan of olive oil.'

'Let her use it for cooking. We will pour desi ghee over dal and subzi before eating it!'

The street vendors with their stalls on bicycles and rickshaws are soliciting customers with their loud announcements. However, a junk dealer has decided to retire his overworked vocal cords and has installed a loudspeaker atop his rickshaw. 'Sell old newspapers! Sell old furniture! Sell old appliances! Dispose of any useless items in your house!' the pre-recorded message resounds through the street tonelessly.

'You must be thinking of selling me off now that he's mentioned the useless items!' Kimti says to Tripta with a wink.

'The raddi wala will be unwilling to pay even a rupee for you! Actually, you are a big liability since you will have to be provided your daily requirement of scotch whisky,' Tripta chuckles.

'Also, medicine and hospital bills,' Kimti adds.

'Anyway, keeping you at home brings me a lot of respect,' Tripta says with a naughty smile.

'Really. I thought you are pitied since you have to spend your life with me.'

'Actually, I am thought of as a sort of "superwoman". Any other woman would have left you long ago!' Tripta exclaims.

Although it is a prickly-worded barb directed at him, Kimti can't help but smile. He reminisces about the era when his writ ran the house and even Tripta had to weigh her words before she used to speak to him. Kimti had built his industrial empire from scratch; he neither had a rich dad nor a rich father-in-law. During his heyday he had been nicknamed 'The Tiger' because he would take insane business risks and because he pioneered the introduction of newer technologies into the automobile parts industry in Ludhiana. Seven years ago, he suffered a major stroke, which left one side of his body paralysed and made him partially lose his speech. Although he recovered fully from it after a long convalescence, it was time to introspect. A signal had rung for him to lead the rest of his life in the slow lane. He decided to divide his industrial empire between his sons and took retirement to lead a life of active merriment.

Though most of his evenings are spent in the bar of the Excelsior Club, today Kimti Lal will be skipping it for the marriage party. Tripta has given up hope of him ever becoming a teetotaller; he has left drinking many times and has invariably started all over again. The longest alcohol-free interval lasted for a month and that too when he was under the spell of a man with saffron robes. She often says, 'He can't remain away from his girlfriend for too long!' He has another girlfriend—Madhubala, the Venus of Hindi cinema. Her posters adorn their bedroom, but Tripti is okay with it.

If Kimti is attending a party where hard drinks are not being served, he doesn't curse the hosts or his luck, unlike some other Ludhianvis. He takes out a small bottle of vodka from his pocket and stealthily pours it into a glass with a fizzy drink. Plus, a full bottle of whisky is always kept in the boot of his car—he calls it 'a spare oxygen cylinder'.

However, he has historically used this bottle for different purposes

- As a weapon during a fight.
- At some parties, the alcohol supply ended too quickly and he was on the verge of losing his mind. The bottle has come to his rescue.
- He has used it as a gift when he has forgotten the actual gift.
- It has also come handy as an emergency bribe.

Soon, both of them are on their smartphones. The old couple have been taught the basics by Lakshya, their technophilic grandson. But when they fumble over simple tasks, he scolds them in the manner of a strict teacher taking a pupil to task. In fact, grandma and grandpa take over most of the bandwidth in the house. Kushal has had to get an extra broadband connection in the house to ensure uninterrupted net connectivity. A 'no internet' situation causes them to feel a 'constriction of chest' and Kushal is worried that it might actually precipitate a heart attack.

Tripta now keeps constant vigil on Kimti and his smartphone because a few weeks ago, he nearly shared his bank account details with online scamsters, thinking that he had won a jackpot in an online lottery. Luckily, he informed Kushal about it and a major loss was prevented. After this incident, Kushal persuaded Kimti to share his passwords. He discovered that Kimti had accepted all the strange Facebook friend requests from pretty women who were not otherwise known to him.

The already droopy corners of Kimti's mouth dropped to his jawline when Kushal told him, 'There is no reason why these stunning ladies should try to befriend an old man when so many eligible young men are around. Most likely, these requests are from men with fake accounts.'

But Tripta also has had her share of gaffes with her smartphone, thinks Kimti. A few days ago, she rang up her sister and expectedly, the conversation went on for half an hour. But the call duration was recorded as three hours since both of them forgot to press the red button to end the call. She has also been left red-faced many a times because of the typos due to autocorrect.

Meanwhile, Reeti is back home from visiting a wedding and lifestyle exhibition; she has never missed even a single of the countless ones that have been held so far in Ludhiana. The organizers of these exhibitions have realized that it is easy to bait the women of Delhi, Chandigarh and Ludhiana by using specific words in their flyers, such as 'latest', 'elite', 'exclusive' and 'fancy'.

Reeti skips her lunch. Instead she pours herself a small bowl of curd and arranges a plate of salad. No, she is not preparing to feast this evening; this is an attempt to make her tummy look as flat as the Indo-Gangetic plain.

The doorbell rings. Shalini, her distant cousin but close friend, enters the living room, holding a leather briefcase. On a closer inspection, Reeti notices the logo. It is Antonio, the Italian luxury brand.

'I don't accept bribes!' Reeti says.

'Good one!'

'Please have a seat,' Reeti says as she conceals a crack in the Italian marble in front of the sofa with her sandal.

'I won't be able to chat with you today, although I am dying to tell you about the latest antics of my husband and brother-in-law. The boot of my car is full of these bulky invitations. I am already behind schedule and I am yet to visit so many women, including those who are suspenseful about whether they would be invited or not. Some of them have been sending daily 'good morning' messages over the last few days, hoping that their names are memorized! Anyway, you have to come with your family, including the senior citizens, by all means,' Shalini says quickly, with an intention to leave.

'I will be there, unless there is some issue at the last moment,' Reeti says although inwardly she feels, '*I too was waiting for this invite with bated breath and I won't miss this wedding at any cost.*'

After Shalini leaves, Reeti opens the briefcase that is also an invitation. Inside are two designer cardboard boxes—one is filled with dry fruits while the other one has heavenly sweets from the iconic sweet maker, Mithaas Sweets. She has to muster her full willpower to avoid eating them; she knows she wouldn't be able to stop at just one.

'*The expenditure of just these invitations must have exceeded the budget of many marriages. Families of Ludhiana are raising the bar or rather, they are crossing all limits. How will a not-so-rich family like ours manage to get our daughter married,*' she worries, but without a frown. The fillers and Botulinum toxin, which she got injected two weeks ago to shine at today's marriage party, have subtracted years from her face, but have also taken away some expressions. When Dr Gayatri, her cosmetologist, told her that she had had enough and more procedures couldn't be carried out on her, she took herself to another doctor and got more treatments done there.

She is dying to show her face to Sapna, her sister-in-law cum bete noire, at the party. Three weeks back Sapna had commented, 'I have noticed that your face has really lost its lustre in the last few months.'

'Oh, it is because of overwork,' Reeti had replied. At that moment she had wished she had the power to curse Sapna and convert her into a toothless witch with countless wrinkles.

For the final touches, Reeti has a booking in the evening at Capri, the most sought-after beauty salon. So, she has no choice but to miss the day's kitty party, which is her favourite. The stars of this kitty are two sisters who precipitate an orgy of laughter with their self-depreciating humour.

After a while Reeti has a periodic urge to check her social media. She comes across her friend, Sohini's post, on Facebook. Sohini has posted a photo of her with Gaganjit, her husband. They are holding hands and looking into each other's eyes as if they are enacting a love ballad. The text reads, 'Fifteen year ago an angel came into my life. Since then, I am living in heaven. You are the most caring and loving husband in this world. I want to be with you for eternity. Happy anniversary to my soul mate.'

Reeti can't help but laugh. *'Lie of the year! She has always described her marriage to me in a single word: loveless.'*

Then she opens up Instagram. After looking at a post, the phone nearly drops from her trembling hand. Binita, whom she follows on Instagram, has posted a picture in an Indo-western outfit, which is an exact replica of the one Reeti is supposed to wear tonight.

A shiver runs through her spine. *'It is quite possible that more copies of the dress could be circulating in the city. What if some other woman turns up at the venue today in the same outfit? We'd both suffer a shock.'*

Sheela, the boutique owner, had told Reeti that this piece was like the Kohinoor diamond, the only one of its kind. Keeping a couple of harsh words pursed in her lips, Reeti calls Sheela. But Sheela doesn't pick up, even after the second or the third call, as if she is expecting Reeti's onslaught. Presuming that she is dodging her, Reeti calls from her mother-in-law's phone. But there is still no response.

She decides to drive down to the boutique to take Sheela to task. An employee of the boutique informs her, 'Madam has gone on a business trip to Delhi where she is planning to open a branch. She might even shift to Delhi and manage the Ludhiana branch from there.'

Reeti mumbles, *'She will soon receive an award for Businesswoman of the Year and I will be in the audience, applauding her. I still remember the day Sheela had started the boutique—in the garage of her home—only three years ago. But the rate at which her business is growing, she will soon think of me as a low-value client.'*

She turns around and goes back home. She calls Binita, after getting her cellphone number through Tanu, their common friend.

'Hello. Reeti here. I am a good friend of Tanu.'

'Good to hear from you. Tanu didi talks a lot about you.'

The Dress of Contention • 79

'Yeah. She is my fan! Okay. There is a major complication. The mauve dress that you are wearing in your Insta post is an exact copy of the dress that I am supposed to wear tonight at a party. Did you get it from Elite boutique, owned by Sheela?'

'I could also say the same thing—that your dress is a copy of mine! I got it from Xtasy. They also told me that it was an exclusive piece for an esteemed client!'

'Are you coming to the marriage party hosted by the Kumars tonight?'

'No, I am leaving for Chandigarh to attend a wedding in the family. But anyway, I will not wear the same dress again because I never repeat party clothes,' Binita says with a flourish. Reeti has met her match.

'That means it is safe for me to wear it today.'

'I don't know. This design might have spread throughout the city like dengue!' Binita quips.

'Oh God! What should I do? Anyway, thanks,' Reeti says and abruptly cuts the call.

Reeti feels like skipping the mauve dress this time and wearing it at some future event instead. But she has talked up this dress among her relatives and friends already; she would have to spend the entire evening explaining what went wrong.

The other option is to wear one of her old dresses. But all of them have been exhibited on social media and there have been panel discussions about them among her friends. If she repeats any one of them at tonight's party, a brash lady could say to her, 'I remember you wore the same dress at such and such gathering.' That would make her wish that the ground opened up and swallowed her whole.

With adrenaline coursing through her body, she sends an SOS signal to her closest friends, Punita and Sahiba. The three of them call themselves sisters and actually support and nurture each other like siblings. Once, Kushal even overheard Reeti revealing family secrets to them. Kushal also suspects that they detail their sex life to each other, uncensored, and that they even compare how well-endowed their husbands are.

'If they make inflated claims, Reeti might get depressed,' Kushal has often considered.

Punita and Sahiba, who live nearby, rush to Reeti's house as if they are paramedics attending to a call for cardiac arrest. Punita, who has light grey eyes, is wearing a loose pyjama with a casual top, while Sahiba's hair makes her look like an escapee from a mental asylum. As soon as she sights them at the driveway, Reeti starts shedding copious tears.

'Baby, if you cry like this for any longer, you could be the world's first case of dehydration because of tears!' Punita says and then hugs her.

Sahiba wipes Reeti's cheek dry with a soft tissue.

Reeti clenches her jaw. 'I feel like shooting Sheela.'

'Cool down. This has happened because your innocent-looking face invites others to take you for a ride,' Sahiba says.

Reeti's face fails to light up at Sahiba's one-liner.

Sahiba continues, 'It may not be the boutique owner's fault. A rogue employee might have leaked the design.'

'What do we do now? File a police complaint?' Reeti asks.

'They have more important matters to tackle, na? Chill yaar.

There is a solution to every problem, except for Kushal's weird dressing sense! We will get you a new outfit right now!' Punita proposes.

'But this one was going to make me the star attraction, next only to the bride!'

Punita raises her voice a bit. 'Just get this dress out of your mind. We don't have much time. I am also attending the celebration at the Kumars tonight. I will lift up your sagging spirits if need be.'

The three of them go to a boutique where the owner is known to Punita. Although none of the designs dilates her pupils, Reeti picks up a piece which she sees as passable. 'Losers can't be choosers,' she says.

The old tailor master wearing thick-rimmed oversized spectacles arrives after an agonizing fifteen minutes. He seems to be a native of Fursatganj. Then he makes up a 'pricey face' and says, 'Not possible to do this task today. Lot of pending work.'

The boutique owner knows the headstrong old man cannot be tackled head on. So she whispers in his ear, 'This lady's husband is a powerful man. Displeasing her might land us in trouble.'

He cowers and gets on with the measurements.

Not willing to take a risk, the ladies stay on at the boutique. Passing time is easy—Minty, a common friend, is such a specimen that they could talk about her without break for a lifetime. When the dress is handed over to them, they rush back. Reeti doesn't head in for a trial as there is neither time nor patience for an alteration.

'It is my destiny,' she says with a sigh.

To cheer Reeti up, her friends make her pick matching sandals and a handbag from a nearby store. Upon reaching home, Reeti rings up Kushal who wonders why she is calling again and again.

'Oh dear! It can't get worse than this,' she cries. 'It seems the Almighty is cross with me. I learnt that the dress I had gotten specially made for the marriage is not exclusive.'

'But you are one in a million! Forget it. Wear an old dress for a change. There are other options too. Rent a dress from some shop or borrow it from a relative or a friend,' the nerd suggests.

'As usual, useless advice! My friends helped me to get a new dress—this is the fastest shopping trip I have ever done! Actually, I shouldn't have talked it out with you. Only a woman can understand what I am going through. Men are blind to the different shades of life, with the exception of spirits, sports and sex!'

'Sort of. But if two men turn up in a similar dress at a party they would just smile and get a picture together! However, for a woman, a dress worth thirty thousand bucks can become worthless, just because it isn't one of a kind.'

'Sorry, honey! I wasted so much money. But the one I got today in lieu of it costed only fifteen thousand rupees. See, I am becoming a judicious spender.'

'Ha ha. Judicious for a day only!' Kushal says and hangs up the phone.

7

Storm Without Warning

Reeti reaches home just in time to receive Lakshya who is alighting from his school bus. As soon as he enters the house, Lakshya lifts his right hand and makes a buzzing sound. He is flying an imaginary aeroplane.

Reeti asks, 'How was your day baby?'

'It was good. Avina celebrated her birthday today. She gave everyone chocolate eclairs. I was the only one who got two,' a beaming Lakshya says.

'Why so?'

'I also give her extra toffees on my birthday!'

'Men will be men! Of course, at different ages they have different tactics,' Reeti concludes.

'What about your tiffin?' she asks him, just like a student who is readying to hear of the exam results.

'I finished everything,' Lakshya says, his eyes downcast.

'Did you eat it yourself or did you give it to someone else?' Reeti asks.

'I ate most of it but Shaurya forcibly took away some stuff,' he says, putting on an innocent face. Reeti is certain that Lakshya took Shaurya's help to finish the tiffin because he didn't want to see the 'doomsday' expression on his mom's face.

Before Reeti can ask him another uncomfortable question, Lakshay rushes to his grandparents' room. The indulgent grandma hands over her smartphone to him.

Lunch is a family affair, minus Kushal, the breadwinner. Reeti pities the poor guy as he has to eat out of a tiffin container. However, she is unaware that Kushal often gorges on drool worthy food, which he has delivered to his factory. Reeti often wonders why Kushal is unable to lose weight despite her acting like Ivan the terrible at the dining table. She presumes that his metabolism is slow, much like his entrepreneurial drive.

'Come on. I won't take you along for the evening's marriage party if you don't finish your lunch,' Reeti says to Lakshya in a tone that reminds Lakshya of the principal of his school. The principal has been nicknamed 'Khatarnak Madam' by him.

Lakshya takes the bait since he always has loads of fun at marriage functions. He can eat anything without his dad classifying it as junk. Also, different marriage avenues provide him with the opportunities to indulge in 'out of the box' pranks.

Ever since Lakshya has added green vegetables to the list of foods which make him say 'yuck', she has had no choice but to resort to trickery. She has pureed boiled vegetables into the gravy of the paneer dish—the vegetables having undergone a cultural revolution similar to the one in Mao's China, losing their individuality for the common good.

After finishing his lunch, Lakshya switches the television on—watching it is as essential for digestion as the enzymes in his gut. He shuns the kids' channels. Instead, he has moved on to *Saagar Apartment*, a family drama. Since he watches lots of soap operas and movies, Lakshya has an adult-like grasp of the nuances of human relationships, especially when it comes to romance. The implication of this soon was obvious to the family a few days ago. Lakshya shouted out a vociferous 'love you' to a cute girl in their neighbourhood, two years older to him. This alarmed the girls' parents so much that they have debarred her from playing with Lakshya. He is the youngest Romeo they have ever come across. Lakshya has a huge crush on Candy Kapoor and if any movie starring her is playing on television, he has to watch it—even if he has done so umpteen times previously.

Sona, the maid, moves to her room when her mobile phone pings. Lakshya follows her stealthily.

When Sona comes back after a few minutes. Lakshya says, 'Mom. Sona was talking to her boyfriend.'

Sona gets an instant blush.

'Bhabhi. I have no boyfriend-voyfriend. I am going to beat up this shaitaan,' she says.

'Catch me if you can,' the little monkey challenges.

Before he gets a chance to make more mischief Shunya, Lakshya's home tutor, enters. Lakshya is instantly transformed into a meek puppy. Shunya looks more like a wrestler than a teacher and has a booming voice to match. After finishing his tuition, Lakshya enthusiastically puts on his skates to go roller-skating at the nearby rink, excited because some lovely girls are among the skaters. Because of them, he has often lost his concentration and slipped.

Reeti has purposely included this chore and made his schedule tighter. She knows that if Lakshya has a lot of time to spare, he makes the house look as if it has been ransacked by a gang of dacoits.

Just before leaving his factory for home, Kushal covers his digital tracks—he removes Diksha's messages, posts and call records. Even Diksha feels that their stealth will ensure that their affair will remain off the radar of everyone, except the all-knowing supreme being who will exonerate them for being human and prone to folly. They control their impulses like professionals and avoid messaging each other after office hours or during the weekend. However, Kushal wouldn't mind even if Diksha crossed the line on social media. Reeti and Kushal have a mutual non-interference pact—they never check each other's mobiles. Also, he has purposely avoided the lock or the pass code on his mobile. His logic is: *'This will convince Reeti that I have nothing to hide.'*

Then, he takes a look at his *Eco Warriors* Facebook page. Only three followers of the group have gotten rainwater harvesting systems installed, while a handful have started with composting. Yes, tree plantation has taken off but the survival rate of the young saplings is low.

'It seems the humble beginnings of our environmental movement are going to remain humble forever,' Kushal grumbles.

As he walks out of the building, he finds his employee wiping off a layer of black soot covering the windshield of his car.

'Alas, there is no way to wipe the soot off the lungs,' Kushal mutters to himself.

The factories belch out black smoke from their chimneys as they use rice husk and coal as fuel, which is often justified by the owners as a necessary evil to cut costs in lieu of the cut-throat competition.

'These guys might be enjoying the surreal atmosphere created by smog.' Kushal imagines them at a party, *'"Hey what a nice smog. Let us clink glasses" they might say.'*

Kushal starts for his home earlier than Reeti's deadline because traffic jams are a routine rather than an exception in the late afternoon. Even though Diwali has already passed, shopping sprees have not let up, a factor which is much loved by the country's economists but abhorred by the green activists.

After he reaches home, Reeti greets him with a kiss which doesn't make him feel like making love to her immediately as is usually the case. *'This kiss was like a sham kiss, the kind film-stars often do while shooting their scenes. It seems like she is still aggrieved about her dress.'*

'I am going to have a short nap. It was a maddening day at the factory today,' he says.

'By the time you get up, a beautician is going to be highlighting my cheekbones at the Capri Salon,' Reeti says as she flicks a lock of hair off her face.

Kushal had expected Reeti to say, *'You deserve the nap because you work so hard to make life easy for all of us.'* But till date, this has never happened. In fact, everyone in the family takes his contribution for granted, just like no one credits gravity for allowing us to sleep peacefully without the danger of being flown away. But even a minor mistake of his is examined under a magnifying lens by Reeti, and even his parents and kids. However, the guests and relatives never tire of praising Reeti.

'She takes such good care of everyone in the family.'

'She is a superwoman; such a great multitasker.'

'She has maintained herself so well.'

'Kushal is so lucky to have her.'

'Thank God, both kids resemble her more than the father.'

'Popsy!' Lakshya shouts from a distance, running towards him. Then he wraps his arms around Kushal's right thigh and feigns as if lifting it. Lakshya likes to give his papa a new nickname every now and then. Previously he has called him 'Peppy', 'Pop', 'Papad' and 'Pappi'.

'Kiddoo, let me sleep for some time. Later, both of us will go to the railway station to receive Vanya and to watch trains,' Kushal tells him.

'Yay!' Lakshya jumps up in the air.

It is an unwritten rule in the house that whenever Kushal goes to the railway station to receive someone, Lakshya has to accompany him, unless the little one is at the school; a breach in this contract involves consequences. Lakshya is so fascinated by trains that on a road trip, he wishes that all level crossings remain closed for hours for him to glance at a train—from the engine to the last bogie. Up until a few months ago, whenever someone asked Lakshya about what he wanted to become, he would reply, 'a train driver'. Reeti made sure to remedy this and hammered it into his mind that he would be better off as a pilot, especially since he would then be able to travel around the world and also overtake all trains in the blink of an eye. Since then, Lakshya calls himself a budding pilot. But even now, the hoot of a muscular railway engine towing multiple coaches is music to his ears.

Kushal takes the stairs to the bedroom on the first floor. He has a special power—to summon sleep at will. Soon, he has a dream and its theme is familiar. He is in Diksha's arms in a hotel room. Since he and Diksha have the whole night to themselves, they play a game—they will arouse each other and whoever becomes impatient will lose. But there is foreclosure of the unlimited foreplay because he feels someone holding his shoulders and shaking them, as if there is a bomb in the house and they have only a few seconds to escape.

'Get up!'

He hears a shout.

Kushal opens his eyes. Everything is hazy at first.

Then Reeti's face comes into view. But he has never seen her like this before. Her eyes have widened, too big for his comfort, and the scowl on her face is similar to what Gabbar Singh had after shooting his henchmen.

Reeti bellows, 'You have always told me that I am the only one for you. "I can't even dream of anyone else ever dislodging you from my heart!" Liar! Cheat! What the hell is going on?'

She throws his phone at him; the screen displays a WhatsApp post that Diksha had sent to him while Kushal was asleep.

'Read this!' Reeti screams.

Kushal's heart rate has doubled in a jiffy. *'Why the hell has Diksha sent a message during the unofficial off-time? And, how mean of Reeti to spy on my mobile?'*

But he is in a bad situation, almost as bad as if he were actually caught in a compromising sexual position with Diksha.

While Kushal was asleep, Lakshya had an impulse to carry out a fresh prank. He ended up checking his dad's mobile. Just a short while before that, Diksha had sent a red rose emoticon to him on WhatsApp. But if Reeti had seen just this, Kushal could have been given the benefit of doubt. However, in addition, Diksha had also texted, relaying it in words. 'I want to take you in my arms. Right now! Waiting for a week will kill me!'

Lakshya wasted no time in showing the message to Reeti, saying, 'Look Mom, Papa has a girlfriend!'

The moment she read the post, Reeti uttered in shock, *'This is for real—this is an affair high on love as well as lust.'* And once she saw Diksha's display picture, she felt like killing her. Kushal's secret girlfriend was attractive enough to enslave him and even make him dump Reeti.

Reeti told Lakshya to go to his room. She didn't want him to witness the impending humiliation of his father.

'I am thankful to Lakshya for revealing your true face to me. Or else I would still be telling everyone that men should learn to control their urges from my husband!' Reeti continues in a betrayed tone.

'Actually...' Kushal tries to explain, '...Diksha is a friend from my college days. She is happily married. There is nothing serious between us.' He clarifies but with his eyes downcast, staring at the floor; he sounds as unconvincing as a playboy telling the media that he has yet to make love to a woman.

'But you are also supposed to be happily married. Does she want you to come to Delhi to take a selfie with her? What if I send such a message to a man and you read it, would you say—"It is okay. I understand. Variety is the spice of life!"'

After listening to this weighty and prickly argument, Kushal's vocal cords go into temporary paralysis.

Reeti continues, 'For the last few days, I have been wondering why you have not been looking at me as lovingly. Now I know. And what a brilliant plan—feigning a business trip!'

Kushal feels like saying, *'My love for you is as deep as it was before. It is just that I have started loving her too!'*

Reeti's eyes become cloudy and soon tears start to stream down her cheeks. Kushal is relieved that her rage has been channelled into her tears. He considers that he has escaped bobbitization and other dangers of kitchen knives.

For the last five minutes, Lakshya has positioned himself just by the side of the entry door. He has overheard everything and has figured out that the fire he has started is getting out of control. Lakshya decides to seek help. He goes to his grandparents' room on the ground floor and says, 'Mom and Dad are having a fight.'

Tripta doesn't even look towards Lakshya and continues to read Facebook posts on her mobile phone. *'Reeti and Kushal's fight is long overdue! Historically, the average time from the initiation of a fight of theirs to the point of reconciliation has been about forty-five minutes. Both of them will feel better after venting their pent-up emotions!'*

'Dada, dadi come quickly with me,' Lakshya continues with an air of urgency.

'What is the issue?' Tripta asks.

'A triangle has formed!'

'What?'

'Like they show in the television shows and movies: two women love one man! And Papa is that man!'

'Let us intervene! This is not a routine fight!' Tripta gestures to Kimti.

Kimti and Tripta take the lift and reach the bedroom on the first floor where they find that an assault is underway. It is not a fight. Reeti is doing all the shouting while Kushal is replying in monosyllables.

Reeti shows the WhatsApp posts to Tripta. 'Mummy ji, your son proclaims himself to be a man of principles. But actually, he is a cheat. I have just discovered that he has at least one secret girlfriend. There might be even more!'

'Mom…I swear, I haven't touched her ever since I shifted back to Ludhiana. We only contact each other on social media,' Kushal says in a low voice.

'If you had not been caught, the certainty of you and that bitch copulating with each other would have been as much as the sun rising from the East!' Reeti interjects.

Tripta looks at Kushal with an expression of exaggerated exasperation. 'Kushal, I am ashamed of you. You have broken her trust. I don't want to listen to any explanations. Apologize to

Reeti and immediately sever all connections with this woman.'

Reeti looks towards Tripta with admiration and considers her anew. *'She isn't blind in love for her son.'* But a wave of emotion overtakes her and she rushes out of the room. Kushal follows her.

Tripta turns her attention to Kimti, 'Since he has a role model like you, this was bound to happen sooner or later.'

'What do you mean?'

Tripta curls her lips. 'You know very well what I mean. A loose character is a trait that runs in your family.'

An old wound has been gouged. Long back, when Kimti was a hot-blooded young man, he had become so enamoured with a young woman that he was almost ready to dump Tripta and the kids. Something similar happened a few years later too.

Still, the slur is beyond Kimti's tolerance. His lips quiver as he speaks. 'Come on. I haven't repeated those mistakes ever again in my life. You can say anything to me. Don't deride my whole family.'

Now, two sets of altercations have begun within the house.

Meanwhile Lakshya goes to his room and bolts the door. He is afraid that his papa will take him to task. Kushal rarely loses his temper but when he does so, he turns into a rowdy man.

'After I marry, I will only love my wife! But no rules before marriage!' Lakshya promises himself.

Reeti and Kushal have returned to their bedroom. Reeti has cooled off a bit, but it is only because of fatigue. Kushal senses a window of opportunity—he tries to take her in his arms. But she pushes him away and gives him the 'I am going to roast you alive' look.

'Don't touch me. This trick of yours has worked previously, but it doesn't stand a chance today!'

Kushal remembers that the most passionate love they have made over the years has been just after their fights.

'Just give me one chance. To tell you the truth, she took the initiative.'

'That's convenient—just like a thief saying that he committed the act while sleep-walking.'

'Please—'

'I should have packed my bags by now; but I don't want to spoil Narinder's mood on such an important occasion. It is no fault of his. Till all the marriage ceremonies are over, I will not mention your "conquest" to anyone, including my parents. I will move out of the house and your life in the morning. Before leaving, I will set your wardrobe in order so that you don't have an excuse to ring me up later on!' Reeti declares.

Kushal fires the last salvo. 'You have to forgive me—for the sake of our kids.'

'The kids will be better off without a father like you!'

Beads of sweat appear on Kushal's forehead despite the mild chill. *'So, she has even planned to keep both the kids with her. Anyway, the kids always side with her, as if they have developed in their mother's womb without the contribution of my sperm!'*

But there is a minor consolation.

Until tomorrow morning, Reeti's hour for dumping him, there *could* be a miracle. Reeti *could* decide to give their marriage another chance. She *could* agree to keep him under a period of 'observation'.

Kushal feels like praying, but isn't sure about the impact since he has never prayed during good times. *'My opportunistic prayers may not cut much ice.'* Suddenly, Kushal senses an opportunity for him to get away from it all, at least for the time being.

'It is time to pick Vanya up from the railway station,' he says.

'Oh! I have an appointment with the Capri salon,' Reeti says quickly and within no time, she is gone.

Kushal types a message for Diksha, 'Our relationship seems to be jinxed. The last message you sent has been read by my wife. As expected, the situation is explosive. For God's sake, don't text me. Anyway, I have no choice but to block your calls and WhatsApp for the time being. I will talk to you after a few days. That is, if I survive this.'

Diksha's replies within a minute. 'Oh my God. It is all my fault. I acted rather immaturely. I will do as you say. Love you loads.'

Diksha's message leaves him even more confused. *'Diksha didn't volunteer that she would never contact me again. What have I gotten myself into? I should have never tried to sail on both boats.'*

Finally, there is a truce between the elderly couple. Kimti, who has forty-eight years of experience in dealing with Tripta's accusations, has managed to quell its resurgent tide.

8

Tense Teens

Kushal knocks on the door to Lakshya's room. Lakshya opens it only after the knocks become more insistent. Kushal fakes a serene face and says, 'Sonny. Let us go to the railway station.'

'I would rather watch TV. I don't want to miss *Tarak Mehta ka Ulta Chashma*,' Lakshya replies, equally serene.

Kushal thinks, *'Lakshya is avoiding me because he fears being the target for the dissipation of my rage. The kid has learnt to put on pretences. The only milestones which I had achieved at his age were speech and toilet training.'*

'Come, baby. Papa is not going to say anything to you.'

'Okay, Papa.'

Kushal whispers to him, 'The lady you thought to be my girlfriend is actually my distant relative. Now don't talk about this to anyone, not even to Vanya.'

'Dad is trying to make a fool out of me. If she is a relative ... why is she expecting him to be in her arms?' Lakshya smiles

knowingly to himself.

'Anything for you, Papa!' he replies like a seasoned diplomat.

Not willing to take a chance, Kushal buys Lakshya a cone of chocolate ice cream, with two extra scoops.

'The cost of bribing him is reasonable at the moment. But when he grows up, God knows what gizmos he will demand.'

Kushal utilizes detours, which enable him to bypass certain congestion-prone traffic lights that test his patience. More often than not, he fails the test. Vanya is even more impatient and creates a scene if he is late even by a few seconds to receive her from the station.

For the last one year, Vanya has been studying at the Green Grove World School at Gurugram, which has become an aspirational brand in Ludhiana, much to the delight of the school management. Reeti wants Vanya to get an IB (International Baccalaureate) degree and then study abroad, and if possible, even settle there. After all, if a family in Ludhiana doesn't have a family member settled across the seven seas they are labelled lethargic.

Vanya is travelling with a group of boys and girls from her school—almost all of them have plans to ditch their hometown later on and settle in other, glitzier towns. They are just in their mid-teens, but they can easily outsmart persons above fifty (whose mental development has been arrested when they were young, as a consequence of watching monotonous shows on Doordarshan). Normally these youngsters indulge in so much gibberish chatter that their co-passengers curse their luck for having been allotted a seat in the same compartment. But today, most of them are quiet, especially the ones that are scared of their parents. These parents tend to have episodes of anger resembling temporary insanity. A week back, these guys and gals underwent a phase of collective insanity themselves, when they got tattooed en-masse. None of them tried to take the consent of their parents prior to the act because the chances of a positive response were in the low single digits.

They have an intense urge to flaunt their tattoos on Instagram and to cause a category five hurricane of appreciation. But they will have to wait till the storms they raise at their homes subside.

Kanan is the most nervous because he decided to get a big dragon tattooed across his arm; fire is likely to be spewed from the mouth of his father who has recently taken a premature retirement from the army. Presently, he seems to be researching on the topic: 'Efficacy of Army Style Discipline at the Home Front'. Sanya's mother has a tattoo on her forearm but she is still likely to be cross with Sanya for not having gone through the proper channel—the parental control portal. Dilpriya is on edge too because she has committed two crimes. In addition to the tattoo, she now has got a coin-sized patch of dark pigmentation on her right cheek. Being an ardent devotee of 'Google Baba', she searched the net for a method to remove a mole on her cheek. She got carried away after reading the post of an individual who suggested the application of ginger-garlic paste. The mole was only partially removed and the innocent skin surrounding was punished instead, for no fault of its own. Despite all this, she is ready to spew venom on anyone who dares to put down the Internet or Google. Like the many female protagonists in epics of love, she takes the full blame on herself to shield her beloved. 'There must have been some fault in my technique,' she says to those who ask.

As they are about to reach Ludhiana, Vanya has a brainwave. 'Hey, let us look up how we can tackle an angry parent. Google or Quora should have a few answers.'

All of them are onboard. But there is nothing on the Internet to add to their pre-existing knowledge on this topic.

'A single key cannot open all the locks,' opines Rajat, the geek. 'All of us have to individualize our strategy in light of our past experiences in dealing with our parents. I am sure all of us have already indulged in acts which have infuriated them to varying degrees.'

Just as he is about to reach the platform, Kushal receives a call from Vanya's cell phone.

'Papa! Where are you? I have been waiting for the last five minutes.' Vanya's rant rattles his eardrums but he understands that impatience is a hallmark of teenagers.

'I checked the train status on my mobile. It arrived on the platform just two minutes ago,' he says.

Kushal's brows rise after finding her with a bright and large gang of boys and girls, who are obviously her schoolmates. *'What is the use of making her study in a world school if she is going to keep the company of kids from Ludhiana? All these kids will do is spread the Ludhiana culture elsewhere!'*

Vanya kisses Lakshya and hands him a chocolate. Then she hugs Kushal.

However, she senses that Kushal is without his half smile,

one which he usually wears for most of his waking hours.

'What is it Pa? Did you have a big fight with mom?'

Kushal is disturbed and pleased at the same time. *'My girl will go far. She has such a good sixth-sense.'*

'Yeah. Sort of. But just routine stuff. It is sorted out now,' he replies. His inner voice has begun to chant. 'Liar Liar,' it says.

'When will the both of you mature!' Vanya smirks.

'Never. We will always behave like teenagers!'

At this juncture, Vanya decides to seize the bull by the horn. 'Dad, I am dying to tell you something. Please promise that you will not be mad at me.'

'This is really smart of her. Asking for a sort of anticipatory bail,' Kushal thinks.

'I have never heard of a responsible father giving his child blanket immunity for all her misdeeds. But I promise I will take a deep breath before saying anything to you,' he assures.

Vanya rotates her left forearm to shows him the tattoo. Simultaneously, she makes a face similar to that of a small-time crook who tries to elicit the sympathy of the judge by stating in the court room that he carried out the snatching to arrange for treatment of his cancer-ridden mother. Vanya has a small butterfly tattoo—which actually looks good on her. This is nothing compared to what his friend Varinder's daughter, Harjasleen, had gotten inked. Kushal spots huge wings all across her small shoulders.

Kushal also remembers that when he was a teen, to demonstrate that his body was producing an adequate amount of testosterone, he had gone to Shimla on his motorcycle, along with another boy—without informing his parents. After he returned, Kimti had demonstrated to him that apart from walking, slippers could be used for other purposes too. Tripta did not intervene. She too wanted solid deterrence against future recklessness on Kushal's part.

'If you had asked permission for a small decorative tattoo, I would have allowed you to go ahead,' Kushal says.

'You are ahead of your times, Papa!' she says, masking her relief.

'But this is your last tattoo. Any more tattoos and everyone will think of you as a weirdo,' Kushal says with a straight face.

'Okay,' Vanya says. She finds some merit in Kushal's diktat, for a change.

The emboldened Vanya has more to add now. 'Papa, you have to fulfil the pucca promise you made to me last month. You said that you would get me an ipad. Please don't say no.'

Kushal is aware that the first quality that Vanya looks for in a new friend is reverence for the image of a partially eaten apple.

'You extracted the promise from me when I was busy in my factory. You already have an iphone and a MacBook,' Kushal says, after recovering from the 440 volts shock.

'But an ipad is also a must-have. Whenever I use my cheap tablet in front of others, I get a huge complex.'

'Vanya, my financial position is tight.'

'Papa, all industrialists say the same! I am not asking for a Porsche! I know you will manage.'

He feels like giving her a discourse on why she should not let status symbols dictate her life but he knows that would be like hitting his head on a wall.

'Give me a day or two to plan the finances,' Kushal says to postpone the inevitable.

After they reach home, the first thing Kushal tries to find out is Reeti's whereabouts. He is happy to know that she hasn't returned home yet. *'Today's party has come to my rescue. If Reeti would have been home the whole day, she would have degraded and shamed me beyond my tolerance. I would have had to run away from this house to an unknown destination. This was likely to be followed by Reeti lodging a police complaint about her missing husband. The media would have gotten a whiff of the kind of story they love the most: about an extramarital affair. It would have been published the next day after being embellished with sleazy details!'*

Vanya rushes to meet her grandparents who are overjoyed to see her. Ever since she has shifted to the hostel at her school, Tripta and Kimti miss her badly because she has always had time for conversations with them unlike Kushal and Reeti who seem to be afraid of receiving unsolicited outdated advice from the elderly.

'How is the young at heart couple?' Vanya greets them.

'Whatever time we have left is a bonus. But, pray that we eat and drink well till the last moment,' Kimti laughs.

'Dada ji, for you only drink is enough to ensure survival!'

'So, how is school?' Tripta asks Vanya, taking the spotlight away from Kimti.

'Dadi, you have regaled me with lots of interesting stories. Over the next few days, I will also tell you about some crazy incidents at school, especially in the hostel. Also, there is a lot to talk about, especially when it comes to my friends. Some of them show extreme deviations from normal behaviour!'

'Good. So what are you wearing tonight for the marriage party?' Tripta asks

'Taking a short break from western outfits. So I am wearing a sharara. My stylo mom has already got it altered for me.'

Lakshya and Kushal join them. Suddenly, Vanya gets up from the sofa and gives Lakshya a cold stare. Then, she speaks in a firm voice. 'Little one. You are not supposed to have an Instagram account until you turn thirteen.'

'What exactly do you mean, Vanya?' Kushal asks. If his ears had active muscles, they would have turned forward.

'He created an Instagram account for himself by *faking* his age. You and mom don't know about it because you don't have any common friends with him. He's smart enough to not use his own name either.'

Kushal thunders, 'Lakshya, the police might catch you for this and put you in jail.'

Lakshya stares at him, his chin raised. 'If they put me in the jail, I will dig a secret tunnel and make good my escape.'

'Get the account deleted, by all means, within a day,' Kushal says to Vanya. Lakshya protrudes his tongue at Vanya. 'I won't tell you my password.'

Kushal positions his right palm in the starting block, readying for a slap. Lakshya knows the threat is now real and his dream of having multiple girlfriends on Instagram will have to wait. But he still has plan B. He will use other social media sites, most of which are 'dark matter' for Kushal or Reeti.

After a brief foray into the brick-and-mortar of her home, Vanya is back on her smartphone. She has opened up five online shopping sites and an equal number of social media sites. During the short break from her smartphone, much has happened on social media: a new follower, a friend request, a proposal worth considering from a cute guy, a laughable proposal from a stupid guy, an entertaining altercation between common friends, likes on her last post reaching three figures, etc.

From the corner of his eyes, Lakshya tries to peep into her smartphone screen.

'Vanya has a boyfriend!' Lakshya suddenly shouts at the top of his voice.

Tripta's eyes open wide. 'How would you know?'

'I saw her sending him a rose from her mobile,' Lakshya says with a mischievous grin.

Vanya remains as cool as a cucumber. 'Grandma, he is bluffing. I actually sent the rose to Simona. She is my best friend.'

Tripta smiles. 'Baby. Are you okay? At this age, you should be sending roses to boys, not to girls!'

'Grandma is so modern and broadminded, so unlike my parents,' Vanya thinks.

'Didi, let us play carrom,' Lakshya says, little realizing that his sister is now out of his orbit.

'Umm. I will play with you tomorrow. I want to chill with my friends today,' Vanya replies.

Lakshya is not used to taking no for an answer. He releases her hair clip and runs away. But she doesn't run after him as she used to and just shouts, 'Kaminey.'

'Yes, I am a Kamina,' Lakshya agrees.

Soon, Vanya leaves for her friends' house where more teenagers are arriving; an impromptu party is almost certain.

Tripta again focuses on the crisis at hand. She comes to the conclusion that she should have been brokering peace between Kushal and Reeti instead of decimating Kimti, a depleted opponent. *'This is the most serious conflict Kushal and Reeti have had to date. It may not be resolved through a simple apology.'*

Tripta and Kimti decide to try and aid them, though they are aware that Kushal and Reeti have rarely valued their advice. They walk up to the couple's bed room where they find Kushal lying on the bed and staring at the ceiling.

'I overheard Reeti saying that she is going to leave you. Is her threat for real?' Tripta comes to the point.

'Most likely. I will be a single man by tomorrow morning, unless the marriage party elevates her mood to such an extent that she decides to give our marriage another chance,' Kushal replies morosely.

'Tell us everything about the other woman in your life. We will try to find some way out,' Kimti chips in.

'The solution will depend on how Reeti reacts. What does it have to do it with Diksha? My parents are being voyeuristic instead of being sympathetic!' Kushal thinks.

'I confess: Diksha is my ex-girlfriend. We became close when I was studying in Delhi and both of us had an intimate relationship.'

Tripta furrows her brows. 'But you never told us at that time.'

'Taking parents into confidence for love affairs was not in fashion at that time! That's why. You too must have hidden quite a few things from your parents in your youth!'

'We didn't consider it at that time. Honestly, we didn't see you as capable of having a girlfriend!' Kimti says with a wry smile.

'Will your girlfriend be willing to leave her husband and kids for you?' Tripta asks.

'Mom has built castles in the air. But she is rather practical.' Kushal thinks. 'Diksha says that her husband is one of the most intellectually-challenged persons she has ever come across but I have a feeling that she is unlikely to leave him because of the kids. From her conversations I could make out that she loves her kids even more than she loves me,' he tells his parents.

'This means that like you, she too is looking for some fun on the side! Have you both had a physical relationship in the recent past?' Kimti asks. His face has acquired the expression of a man watching porn.

'Not at all. We have only talked on phone or chatted on social media.'

'Poor guy. Got caught without even enjoying himself!' Kimti chuckles.

Tripta grimaces at Kimti. 'Just keep quiet. We have such a difficult situation at hand and you are cracking jokes.'

Kimti's smile does a disappearing act. The man who was once nicknamed 'tiger' deserves a new nickname—'domesticated cat'.

9

Sequential Troubles

In the fracas that ensued in the house, Reeti believes she has missed her appointment at the salon.

As soon as Kushal leaves for the railway station to bring Vanya home, she commands Satyavan, the chauffer, 'Take me to the salon quickly—like a fire brigade driver who has to reach the site of a major fire. Consider that a number of lives are at stake.'

She has never behaved like this with Satyavan. Since he thrives on a diet of crime shows, he feels sweaty.

'If I am not able get her to her destination on time, she will hurt me... she might use her long fingernails to scar me forever or even strangle me with the strap of her purse,' he shudders as he remembers the oft repeated dialogue of Chintan, the moustached anchor from the crime serial, *Jaagte Raho*, 'Often, heinous crimes are not committed by criminals but by seemingly normal folk.'

Satyavan drives. He presses down on the horn almost non-stop. The cyclists and two-wheeler drivers save themselves by swerving to their left. But they blurt out practiced curses, hoping that they will seek out the offender, like a guided missile. However, an elderly man with a 'turn the other cheek' type of mentality mutters loud enough for Satyavan to hear, 'Oh God. Please grant sanity to this mad driver.'

As soon as they reach the Capri Salon, Reeti bellows, 'I am screwed', much to the amusement of her chauffer. She has noticed quite a few cars parked in front of its fancy interiors and even in the adjacent areas.

After gathering her wits, she reasons, *'Oh, I see. Auspicious days for marriages are auspicious days for salons too.'*

Her chest is heaving as she enters the salon. Usually, Sasha, the angelic lady at the front desk and the de-facto brand ambassador of the salon, gives her a welcome befitting a queen. Reeti is their prized customer, one who is amenable to manipulation if simply showered with enough adoration. However, Sasha pouts at her today, as if Reeti is a trespasser.

'Sorry, madam,' the receptionist says. 'You missed the appointment by an hour.'

'There was a medical emergency at home,' Reeti says, trying to strategically use the politicians' favourite excuse, the sympathy factor.

'I can't help it. We are already overbooked right now. All of our beauticians are so busy that they are on a forced fast.'

Reeti mutters to herself, *'That adulterous bitch is directly or indirectly responsible for whatever is going wrong in my life today.'* But she isn't one to admit defeat easily. 'I am your regular client. You have to adjust and seat me by all means.'

'So are the ones who are being attended to! Madam, I would have accommodated you on any other day. But today we have had to turn back many regular clients like you already. I have heard a lot of curses. Even if a single one of them rings true, I might turn into an old witch!'

Sasha's attempt to defuse the tension with humour doesn't work with Reeti. Her expression remains grimly grim.

'Let me talk to Saundarya, your owner. She knows me quite well.'

'Sure.'

Reeti calls Saundarya only to find her phone switched off. *'I am sure she is hiding in a panic room, ignoring calls from many other desperate women today!'*

She has no alternative but to try her luck somewhere else. Then, her jaw drops. She sees a lady walking out after her makeover. After the second look to confirm, Reeti comes to the conclusion that she can't call herself the unofficial 'Mrs Ludhiana' anymore. Her ego has crashed like a shoddily constructed building after an earthquake.

'I have never spotted her on social media or at a party or even a lifestyle exhibition. Either she is a newcomer to the city or she is a freak who doesn't socialize,' Reeti presumes.

To add insult to the injury, the femme fatale gives Reeti an icy stare, like a blue-blooded queen looking down upon a courtesan. Reeti feels like scrubbing grease into her hair, smudging her lipstick and tearing her dress.

The day is as bad as it gets. A visit to another salon proves futile. They are downright rude. 'During the wedding season, we don't just entertain anyone who enters from the street!'

'Behave yourself. I can easily buy out your salon,' bellows Reeti, although she knows all she can afford is their furniture. Before the receptionist can retort, she walks out.

She has no choice but to turn to her twenty-four by seven lifeline: Reeti calls her mom.

'Mom, I have been eagerly waiting for this day for the last so many months. But I am facing one disaster after the other today,' Reeti howls in between sobs.

'What happened, my sweetie?'

'I will tell you the details later but right now I urgently need to get my hair styled and make-up done. The last two salons that I visited simply kicked *me* out.'

'Why don't you just wear some lipgloss and eye-liner. Tell everyone that minimal make-up is in vogue now. Search for a French actress whose name is a tongue-twister. Call it her signature style.'

'Mom, I am in the midst of a panic attack and you are trying to be funny!'

'Relax. I have thought of a solution. Since even freelance make-up artists will be busy today, our only option is a home beautician. I know of a lady who does home visits. Just go back and cuddle with Kushal! I will coordinate it.'

'Kushal has left such a goody-goody impression on everyone that even Mom won't believe that he has a girlfriend on the sly. I will tell her everything once the marriage is over,' Reeti says to herself, still sobbing.

Reeti reaches home. She can't believe that Vanya has already left for her friend's home without a hello. *'She could have waited for me. Nothing is going right. Despite caring so much for everyone in the family, I am losing them to outsiders!'*

In the living room, she comes across Kushal. Bracing himself for another round of fireworks, he avoids eye contact and keeps his gaze glued to the screen of his mobile phone.

'What time do we leave?' Reeti asks out loud. She seems placid, at least for the moment. *'I shouldn't be lulled into complacency. This is just the lull before the storm,'* he reminds himself.

'Around eight,' Kushal replies. 'Right now, I am going to the marriage venue to help Narinder in overseeing arrangements. I will be back by half-past-seven.'

'Okay,' Reeti says. She isn't worried about Kushal taking long to get dressed. Most likely, he will simply slip on the black shirt with its collars as long as the ears of a rabbit and pair it with pleated white trousers, a combination that has expired thirty years ago. His vintage blazer will enhance his eccentricity further. Kushal doesn't have any other saving graces either—the angular jaw, rippling biceps or a washboard stomach.

While Kushal is away, Reeti decides to coach Lakshya.

'Laksh, don't talk about the WhatsApp message you saw on Papa's phone with anybody.'

'Okay, Mom. I don't want Papa to have a girlfriend because you are my BFF. So I told you everything.'

Reeti plants a kiss on his forehead.

'In the event of a battle between me and Kushal, he will surely be on my side.'

10

Show Show and More Show

On the way to Maharani Palace, the wedding venue, Kushal can't help but satirize Ludhiana's weddings, prickly thorns in his life.

'People from Ludhiana will be amongst the first to hold marriage ceremonies on the moon and Mars once human colonies are set up there and commercial space flights become available. However, there could be many complications arising from this development. Ludhianvis would insist that scotch whisky be served during the space flight along with tandoori chicken. The women would have embroidery done all over the drab space suits. Also, they would expect the décor of the wedding venue to change with every celebration.'

Kushal knows of three outlandish weddings, after which the couples separated within a year; crores of rupees went to waste, as if they were simply burnt as a fuel in a fireplace. A few years ago, divorce was rare; marital conflicts were sorted out with the help of relatives and friends on special duty. These counsellors could iron out differences with such finesse that the couple felt guilty of having acted immaturely. Later on, they were given the status of 'honorary adviser' by the couple and continued to be their on-call troubleshooters. But, nowadays, for many men and women, adjustment ends at adjusting the volume of their earphones and any kind of advice is anathema to the 'it's my life' dictum of their generation. Even love marriages don't bring any succour for the parents as they are celebrated in more or less the same way, where the instant generation make sure to fulfil the need of their Instagram moments.

Kushal has tried to convince a few relatives and friends to prepare for a no-frills marriage for their daughters. The money saved could be invested in their daughter's name too, making her a queen in the long run and not just on the wedding day. But, instead of being grateful to him for giving them such valuable advice, they have taken this as a frontal attack on Ludhiana's social and cultural fabric. Some people have even unfriended him on social media. He has developed a great respect for social reformers, realizing how much resistance they must have faced in their times.

However, some green shoots are visible.

A wedding is in the news because a high-profile family has solemnized it with twenty-two family members, eleven each, from the bride's side and the groom's. But instead of applauding this step, relatives and friends are spreading word that there must be some major 'defect' in either the bride or the groom.

'The families might have also received threats from members of Ludhiana Money Culture Society,' Kushal smiles.

Kushal is so relieved that this event is the last ceremony

on the bride's side. During the ring ceremony, the mehndi, the sangeet and the cocktail night, he has imbibed more alcohol than plain water, and his food intake has exceeded the diet of a sumo wrestler. Kushal's excesses have broken their own record. Yesterday, Dr Angrez Singh, his friend, warned him: 'Excessive intake of alcohol damages not just the liver but also the brain, the pancreas and the heart.'

He has mixed feelings about this piece of information. *'I wish I didn't have to know this and had continued in the accepted mode: "eat drink and be merry, especially when others marry".'*

Kushal enters the venue. As expected, activities have taken on a feverish pitch to give the final touches. Workers are setting up a gazebo at the entrance, moving at heights with as much ease as his arboreal ancestors. Their only safety device is the good karma of their previous birth. The burly supervisor, with a handlebar moustache and betel-stained teeth, addresses these workers by invectives rather than names.

Kushal is amused. *'The workers don't seem to mind his language. Probably they will faint out of shock if he is kind to them or if he addresses them as bhai saab.'*

He enters the office of the resort where Narinder Kumar, the host, is having a meeting with Ajiteshwar Singh, the marriage palace owner. They are trying to iron out the wrinkles in their financial arrangements. Kushal is known to him too. Narinder is wearing a metallic blue suit with a black tie and this seems to be his full and final outfit for the evening.

'So? All set for tonight?' Kushal inquires.

'Yes. Everything should go smoothly.' Ajiteshwar Singh says, moving his executive chair like a pendulum. 'From experience we know that most of the untoward incidents happen in the latter part of the event, when people exceed their drinking capacity. Kushal, alcohol is our best friend and also our biggest enemy!'

'Please note down my mobile number. If you find an old man with henna-dyed hair causing trouble, just call me. I'm certain that will be my dad!' Kushal smiles.

Ajiteshwar and Narinder laugh out loud at this heartfelt joke.

'So, how is the business?' Kushal asks Ajiteshwar.

'It is good. Thankfully, getting married is still in fashion! But just a few days are left for this marriage season. After that, our star will dip, auspicious days will be over and only a few bold souls will dare to solemnise their marriages.'

'I can convince you that astrology is a pseudo-science. But for that we need at least a half an hour session,' Kushal says, in an authoritative tone. Like crocodiles waiting to pounce on the wildebeests in the Mara river of Kenya's grasslands, he is always looking for opportunities to tear astrology down to shreds. Kushal has even written an article for the *Scientific Temper* magazine, titled, 'Sun Signs are Fallacious'.

'Well, I beg to differ. Astrology is among one of the greatest disciplines! The concept of auspicious days causes a mismatch between demand and supply and helps us jack up our rates for that period,' Ajiteshwar says with a wink.

Kushal is in familiar territory. 'If a scientific study is conducted comparing the success of marriages solemnised on auspicious and inauspicious days, I am sure that the difference wouldn't be statistically significant.'

'Please keep your disruptive ideology to yourself! Think of the people employed in the wedding industry. They have mouths to feed.'

They all laugh and Ajiteshwar continues, 'Okay, if you make peace with astrology, I will give you a special discount whenever you choose to have your daughter's wedding.'

'A nice bribe to buy my silence! I may make a lot of noise about having simple marriages but it seems I too will have an ostentatious ceremony when it comes to my daughter. If I refuse, my wife will either murder me or commit suicide, depending upon which of the biochemicals in her brain are predominant that day.'

Then, the husband-and-wife team, in the form of the wedding planners called Karan and Sayesha, enter the office. Both of them are dressed in casuals. But their Patek Philippe watches are a testament to the fact that they may choose to retire to a villa in Goa whenever they feel like and even support their future generations if they turn out to be bad at this business.

'Meet Kushal, my brother-in-law. He is one of the brainiest persons in Ludhiana!' Narinder introduces.

They greet Kushal but don't initiate any conversation with him—the male equivalent of a plain jane isn't a potential client. In fact, he doesn't seem to have the DNA of a Ludhianvi in him, they notice.

They turn to Narinder. 'Mr Narinder, the wedding party, including the groom, will be bowled over by the decoration after entering the pandal. As you know, everything, from flower arrangement to table linen is exclusive—we never repeat any of our designs! Your daughter's wedding is going to be talked about for a very long time. And the social media section of our company will make this auspicious news so viral that your phones will be flooded with likes and comments.'

'Unique, Showy, talk of the town. They know these words inflame neurons in the Punjabi brain,' Kushal mutters to himself.

Together, they leave the office and enter the main venue.

The wedding planners continue to rave and rant about their exclusive décor and the colour palette. Kushal has no choice but to use a few superlatives to cheer Narinder up. He also makes a few suggestions, which are rubbished by the wedding planners who seem to believe in the dictum that celebrity wedding planners don't take any advice. Finally, Kushal leaves—rather, escapes—providing the excuse that he has to pick up his daughter from her friend's house.

11

The Beauty and the Beautician

Reeti's face lights up as the doorbell rings and Rosa, the home beautician, enters. Rosa is taken to the guest room on the ground floor of their spacious house.

Her smile is too wide for Reeti's comfort. *'She can't be labelled beautiful in the eyes of the beholder of any culture, race or nationality,'* she considers unkindly.

Rosa has brought along an equally odd-looking, fumble-prone assistant who opens a suitcase full of glossy equipment.

'You have such a great skin. You must care for it a lot and must also have a superb diet,' Rosa says. Reeti understands that she is being primed with flattery but she doesn't mind—it gives her an even greater kick than a Tequila shot.

She smiles and says, 'Apart from a meticulous diet, I also work-out regularly and socialize a lot.' She feels like adding that she has a good sex life but checks herself.

'Okay, what do we begin with?' Reeti asks.

Rosa tries to strike gold straightaway. 'A gold facial would make your face shine like anything.'

'Gold is an inert metal and is unlikely to have any effect at all on the skin,' Reeti says with the air of a scientist. Actually, this fact has been conveyed to her by her nerdy husband. Rosa blinks copiously. *'Most ladies are so enamoured of the word "gold" that they easily give in to my suggestion. In fact, none of them has ever countered with a scientific explanation.'*

Reeti tells Rosa, 'See, we have no time for a facial or even for a peel-off mask. Just get on with the hair styling and the make-up.'

'How many kids do you have madam?' Rosa asks, readying her brushes.

Reeti chuckles, 'When I am in this house, everyone acts like a kid!'

Reeti is good at reading people. *'Rosa is trying to develop a relationship with me to build the foundations of a long-term relationship. Next, she is going to address Kushal as bhaiya and my mother-in-law as mummy ji.'*

Her suspicion is confirmed when Rosa says, 'If you are so occupied with taking care of everyone, it is better that instead of going to the salon, you call me home. This will save your time as well as your money.'

Reeti dangles a juicy carrot in front of Rosa. 'Do your best. Since I have a huge circle of friends, I can give you lot of references.'

It takes a good ten minutes for Rosa and her assistant to set up the equipment, courtesy a faulty cable and a few fumbles because of Reeti acting like she is Mrs Hurry.

Meanwhile, Lakshya enters the room.

'Mom, who is she?' he asks.

'She is a beautician; she will do the hairstyling and make up for me.'

'I also want to get my hair styled and my make up done.'

'Only the girls get this done. Have you ever seen a male actor wearing a bright red lipstick?'

'I want to be a girl too. They wear such nice dresses.'

'But usually only boys become pilots.'

'Then, I want to remain a boy only,' Lakshya announces. 'What is this?' Lakshya asks after a few minutes, toying with the idea of using the kit of the beautician as his toy for the day.

Reeti can't afford any more interruptions.

'Lakshya, go away or else I will give you a tight slap.'

Lakshya sticks his tongue out at Reeti and runs away.

Reeti shows Rosa a picture of hers, taken at a recent party, to make Rosa's job easy. Rosa puts her heart and soul into her hair styling but Reeti gives her an empty stare—she seems to be fixated on the styling that her regular salon is able to create on a consistent basis.

'Okay, leave the hair as it is. Try your luck with the facial make-up!'

By now, fear of failure has made Rosa's skill nosedive to the level of an apprentice. She uses the wrong shade of foundation.

Reeti studies her face in the mirror: the job is below par. Once again, she has no choice but to accept her 'fate'.

Reeti pays the professional charges to Rosa and tepidly mutters a 'thank you', which to Rosa, sound like a command to 'get out'. Rosa gets even, in her own way: she doesn't give her contact number to Reeti before leaving.

'These maharanis don't feel satisfied until they part with a big chunk of their money at a high-end salon. I neither want to work on her nor on her friends, who are going to be as snooty!' she says to her assistant right outside Reeti's house.

Vanya returns home to find Reeti sitting on the sofa in the living room. Reeti gets up in a flash. Their high-decibel cries are followed by hugging with a force equivalent to the grip of a python.

She notices Vanya's tattoo.

'What an amazing tattoo. It must be temporary?.'

'No, Mom. It is permanent,' Vanya says.

'Everyone in this house is getting out of control,' Reeti sneers, although in her heart of hearts she feels like getting a similar tattoo.

'Who else Mom, apart from me and Lakshya?' asks Vanya.

'We will talk about that later,' Reeti replies quickly.

Reeti puts on the dress that she had got stitched earlier in the day to salvage her pride. But she feels like crying after she looks at herself in the mirror. It is loose at the most critical area, the waist, laying to waste all the gym visits and all the times she has curbed her temptations in the past few months.

'The old tailor seems to have reached a stage beyond 'experienced'. He is senile,' she whines to herself.

Although she has a more than an ample bosom, Reeti still puts on a padded bra; she likes to 'project' her 'soft' power.

Then she puts on the piece de resistance, the necklace which she purchased after tormenting quite a few salespersons in many jewellery showrooms. Not to be left behind, her chittiyan kalayian seek her Cartier watch. Its time mechanism is out of order—courtesy Lakshya. But till date, no one has ever asked her, 'what is the time now' at these parties.

Finally, she squirts on her favourite Chanel perfume, wherever her hand can direct the spray. Lakshya also forces his mom to spray some on him. He is wearing brand new jeans and a t-shirt; he too doesn't repeat a dress at parties, making Kushal feel gloomy about the future of his beloved planet. Vanya is wearing a sharara for the first time and has blocked the main mirror of the dressing area for the last ten minutes. In trying to admire herself from different angles, she has developed cramps in her neck; she wishes it was as flexible as the neck of an owl.

Kushal reaches home well in time and gets ready in the blink of an eye. Reeti too is in the last lap of her marathon makeover session; she is wearing her sandals.

'Oh my god,' she squeals.

'What happened? Did you see a cockroach?' Kushal asks quickly.

'No. My sandals are not matching at all with my dress. While I was buying them, they looked perfect.'

Kushal squints his eyes but can't find any appreciable difference in the shade of her sandals and her dress. *'Without this colourful character called Reeti, my life would be colourless!'* he exclaims to himself.

'Sometimes the hue of lights in the showroom can lead to

a different perception of colour,' Kushal says with a poker face.

'The truth is that the salesman in the showroom pulled a fast one on me. He belonged to your category: an expert in deceit!'

Kushal feels like rebuffing her but checks himself and plays it safe. 'Quite possible. But you could wear sandals which are contrasting in colour with your dress. I am sure there must be some in your collection.'

'You can give these ideas to Diksha!' Reeti says, leaving Kushal speechless.

'If an award is instituted for the worst-dressed woman at the celebration, I stand a good chance of winning it,' she feels

Lakshya's itch for mischief has resurfaced. Just as everyone seems to be on the starting block to leave, Lakshya takes out an ice cube from the refrigerator and puts it on the back of the maid's neck, and it slips under her dress; gravity, and not Lakshya, is the executor of the prank. For most of its journey, it is beyond the reach of her hands. By the time she is able to catch the cube from her lower back, it is reduced to the size of a pea, most of it having melted. Usually, Sona enjoys Lakshya's pranks but this one, since it comes with a annoyingly cold ice cube and a wet dress, makes her lose her cool. She sulks and sits in a corner.

Reeti puts a hand on her shoulder. 'Sona, he is just a kid and you are so mature. Come on, ignore him.'

'No, he is not *just* a kid. Sometimes he talks even more sensibly than you!' she grumbles.

It takes another five minutes for Reeti to calm Sona down.

Meanwhile Kushal happens to glance at the wall clock and realizes that the family should have been rubbing shoulders with men and women in demonstrative attire under bright lights by now. On any other day, he would have taken it as an opportunity to yell at Reeti and the company, but today he talks in the tone of a sycophant addressing his boss, 'Reeti, please hurry up. Family members should reach earlier than the formal guests.'

But he knows his nudge is like the first hoot of the railway engine. It will take a minimum of three to four such exhortations to manifest in a result.

As he had feared, Reeti and Vanya can't resist a mini photo session.

'If I was a lady who discovered a few hours ago that my husband had been unfaithful, I wouldn't even be in the mood to go to a celebration, let alone being photographed,' he thinks.

Reeti and Vanya try various combinations of smiles, pouts and other facial postures to strike a pose. Kushal clicks the picture and shows it to them for their approval with bated breath.

Vanya shakes her head. 'Poor click, Dad! Do it again.'

He'd forgotten to switch the flash on.

Lakshya snatches the phone from his Dad and changes the settings. 'Papa, you are a gone case! You don't even know this!'

'Sorry, sir,' Kushal says in a childish tone, making Lakshya giggle.

'Okay. You take the photo,' Kushal continues. He lifts him up to provide him with a good angle for the click.

Then Vanya tells Kushal and Reeti to pose together. Both of them stand calmly, making sure to leave a small gap between them. They make sterile poses, as if they are being made to smile at gunpoint.

'Come on, Papa, put your arms around Mom as you always do. And why are you guys being so miserly with your smiles?' Vanya cajoles.

Kushal and Reeti try their hands at acting.

'I always tell my friends that my parents set the benchmark for an ideal couple,' Vanya says in a mushy voice.

Kushal's sham smile terminates quickly.

'Vanya will be shattered once she finds out that her dad has such a loose moral character, even by today's standards. What sort of an example am I setting for her?'

The photos are posted on various social media accounts. The likes and comments immediately begin to accumulate. Some of Reeti's friends seem to be online with the alacrity of a hungry kingfisher perched on a branch at the edge of a lake, waiting to pounce.

12

Reaching Marryland

After everyone has taken their favourite seats in the black Mercedes, Kushal announces, 'All of you think over it one last time. Are you missing something? I am not going to turn the car midway to the party.' His patience is now lost. It has been wearing thin for quite some time now.

But Kushal has avoided taking along his metallic water bottle, which symbolises his opposition to disposable plastic water bottles because this is a sore point between him and Reeti. He can't afford to enhance Reeti's already elevated level of rage.

The invitation card shows 8 p.m. as the time for the reception of the baraat—but the word 'sharp' is purposely not mentioned. In no one's living memory has any baraat in Ludhiana reached on the dot.

Kushal is reminded of the wedding of his cousin's daughter a few years ago. She had been won over by the son of a retired brigadier. On the wedding day, the hosts were afraid that if the groom and his entourage reached on time, of which there was a distinct possibility, the baraat would be greeted by an empty venue. In such a case, Brigadier Sahib could declare the bride's family to be foes, subject them to verbal firing and call off the marriage. So, the groom's parents were specifically instructed on the day of the marriage to respect the I.S.T. (Indian Stretchable Time) of civilians and be substantially late. The brigadier had to profusely apologize to his principles.

Today, the traffic is smooth and the vehicles flow on the highway. There have been instances where the bride or the groom had to be taken to the venue on scooters because of intractable traffic jams in Ludhiana.

Tripta initiates a conversation. 'The boy is not so good looking.'

'But for boys, it is the financial position which matters the most. Moreover, saadi kudi (our girl) is also slightly on the healthy side,' Kimti adds.

Reeti smiles to herself. In Ludhiana, an overweight person is referred to as 'healthy' while a person with normal weight is labelled 'weak'.

Kushal tries his hand joining the gossip. 'I have heard that Narinder is spending a lot of money on dowry—hundred tolas of gold, an undisclosed amount of cash, along with a super car and a factory. Mercedes cars are also being gifted to some members of the groom's family.'

'I wish we were from the groom's side. We could have gotten rid of this old Mercedes,' Kimti jokes.

As they reach the Maharani Resort and alight from their car, Kushal hands over the key to an attendant for valet parking.

Although valet parking is convenient, this can be a complication for those who own small cars and bother too much about what others are thinking about them—someone or the other will be able to notice the vehicle you have arrived in.

A brand-new Audi stops behind them. Familiar faces emerge from it. Vishesh, Kushal's cousin, along with Manya, his wife.

Reeti feels like scratching their car. *'How could these chaps buy an Audi? Just a year ago the condition of his family business was like that of a patient on a ventilator.'*

Vishesh had joined his family business after he was laid off from his job in Pune in an engineering firm. However, he turned it around by taking risks, which were otherwise labelled by his father as too foolhardy; his father had to eat his words later on.

'Vishesh has either started smuggling something or has become a drug dealer—there can be no other explanation for his quick rise,' Reeti can't help commenting.

'While she expects likes and compliments in wholesale, she should learn to appreciate others once in a while,' Kushal feels.

Then, 'oohs' and 'aahs' escape from every mouth. A Bentley, bedecked in flowers, is parked in front of the entrance—at an appropriate vantage point—so that everyone gets the message that in the Kumar household, money is not counted but weighed. It is also an indicator that the party is going to set new benchmarks in town. Obviously, the Bentley is a humble gift to the groom from the bride's family.

Next, a sign with the words 'Nancy weds Shobhan', greets them in calligraphic font. The bride's nickname is Mitthi while the boy is lovingly called Laddoo. But 'Mitthi weds Laddoo' would have read like the name of a fusion sweet cooked by a celebrity chef. So, their proper names have been printed. In fact, when the wedding cards reached the relatives, a few of them were flummoxed; it was the first time that they learnt of the proper names of their nieces and nephews.

The entrance area, decorated with flowers in intricate vases and chandeliers, has been purposely made circuitous to let the guests know that the show of this event is to be the showiest.

Reeti's neck is moving in as many directions as its range of motion allows. 'How lovely these flowers look. Especially the purple orchids.'

Kushal gives a low amplitude nod. This disappoints her. These blossoms haven't exactly induced him to compose a couplet in their praise. Just a week ago, he read an article about intensive floriculture—these beautiful flowers hide some ugly secrets, which includes the extensive use of pesticides.

As they are walking down a small carpeted staircase leading to the main venue, Reeti falls on him. Kushal realizes that that it is not a show of affection—she has lost her balance, probably because of the newly purchased high-heeled sandals, which have yet to form a close relationship with her feet. Reeti says with a poker face, 'Thanks. I would have sprained my ankle but for you.'

'Such tepid gratitude. She isn't thawing, not even a bit,' Kushal thinks.

Narinder and his wife, Kaajal, the hosts, are standing at the entrance to welcome the guests along with some uncles and aunties. The youngsters are conspicuous by their absence though one day, they will be in the same category.

Narinder looks towards Kushal. 'Why so late dear? Did you spend a lot of time in the beauty salon?'

'Yes. A manicure and pedicure were long overdue!' Kushal laughs.

The photographers at the entrance take their job very seriously. They don't 'okay' the click with the hosts until the guests sport a thousand-watt smile.

The main venue is flooded with lights of various hues from large and small lamps whose number exceeds that of the stars in the sky. Wires bearing them have been entwined with the surrounding trees too. Kushal imagines, *'If an alien ship was planning to land, its pilot might zero in on this area because it would appear as one of the brightest spots on earth.'*

Reeti stands still for a while. She is transfixed by the turquoise and blue themed décor.

But Kushal is gritting his teeth. *'What a waste. Humans are digging their own grave.'*

Soon, all of them settle on the special sofa seating in the central area.

Quite a few guests have arrived but more arrivals are expected past 10 p.m. Of course, there are people who have a reputation of reaching near midnight, when most guests have already left the venue; some of them are *actually* short on time, while the others feign that they are short on time.

The Rahejas look at each other. They are not able to initiate much conversation. All they do is sample the different snacks with fancy names carted around by over-attentive waiters. The rosti turns out to be a cousin of the aloo tikki while the Thai

Bomb is paneer tikka in disguise.

Slowly the group starts to scatter. Lakshya is the first to make a move. 'Mom, I want to play.'

'But this venue is so huge. After a while, there will be hundreds of people and it will be difficult to find you.'

Lakshya thinks about this for a moment.

Reeti expects him to come up with a bright idea, such as 'If I can't locate you, I will request someone to let me call you from their mobile phone.'

But Lakshya delivers something else. 'I will tell the DJ to announce that the mother of Lakshya has gotten lost! If she is listening, she should come near the DJ station.'

Reeti's nostrils flare. 'Don't you dare do that. Simply locate Papa near the drinks counter!'

The thing Tripta loves the most about these gatherings is that almost everyone younger to her bows to her and touches her feet—it is another matter that they don't listen to her anymore. However, she is missing the beat of the dholak and the traditional wedding songs, a melody for which her relatives flocked once upon a time.

'*Bollywood, the cultural monster, is gobbling up so many traditions,*' she laments.

Another septuagenarian couple joins them and the conversation veers towards married life, specifically its oddities.

Suddenly, Kimti gets up from his seat and gestures. 'During her lifetime, Tripta has spent double the time with me as compared to her parents. Still her loyalties lie with her parents and siblings!'

Everyone smiles.

Jeevan, Kimti's friend, adds, 'Almost every husband feels the same way. In fact, when I was newly married, my father-in-law had told me, "A wife will tolerate a lot of her husband's nonsense but if he denigrates her parents or her siblings, she will surely turn into a ferocious bitch!"'

Charu, his wife, can't hold herself back. 'You haven't done even a fraction of what my parents have done for me. You know very well that once upon a time I was the talk of the town. So many boys were after me! But I was destined to end up with you.'

Jeevan swells his chest. 'Ha ha. I didn't kidnap you. Your family pestered my parents. By the way, I was also a highly eligible bachelor and one girl even threatened to commit suicide when I refused to marry her. I did that for you.'

Sumitra, a cousin of Tripta, happens to pass by. Tripta reluctantly greets the woman who has been nicknamed 'search engine' since she makes a hobby of peeping into the lives of others.

She stares at Vanya for a long time. 'Wow. The little girl has grown up. Start planning for her marriage well in time!'

Vanya feels like retorting with something sharp but she remembers her grandma's advice. 'Most people above the age of seventy start behaving in an odd fashion and one shouldn't take their utterances to heart—including that of her own grandparents!'

Vanya keeps mum.

'I am so eager to marry off my darling daughter in style that I might do it as soon as she turns eighteen!' Reeti says out loud, although she is aware that it is her wishful thinking. Vanya is still quiet and ambitious—she will first marry her profession and think about the other marriage later on.

As Vanya had expected, Sumitra passes a judgement about her body.

'Beta, you have become weaker than before. Are you eating a proper diet at the hostel? As long as you are at home, eat well.'

Vanya nods in the affirmative but she feels, *'The so-called weak girls are actually the stronger ones; they get all the modelling contracts and acting roles!'*

Vanya spots a friend and moves out of the danger zone. Soon, her gang of friends are all together. She shows them her tattoo, and for the next fifteen minutes, they talk about celebrities and *their* tattoos. However, she warns them not to copy her action blindly; her parents were unusually accommodative, theirs might not be the same.

Lakshya is happy to explore the marriage venue on his own. He knows that accompanying adults spoil all the fun by trying to make him behave like them. He surveys the stalls serving snacks and is fascinated by the sushi and the caviar on display.

But he wonders why hardly anyone is eating it. *'I will try it when I become a big boy!'* he assures himself.

He plays it safe and locates the pizza station. After devouring a big cheesy slice of pizza, he looks for some action. As he wanders, he comes across a sweet little girl whose parents are busy conversing with a couple. He tiptoes behind her, pulls her braid and by the time she is able to turn around and look, he hides behind the legs of a heavy-set man.

Instead of her wails and cries, Lakshya hears her bellowing.

'Coward, face me,' she says.

He shifts a bit until she is in his field of vision; she has struck a karate pose.

His jaw is agape. *'If she had caught me, she would have done to me what heroes do to the bad guys in movies. Am I the bad guy?'*

Then, he notices a drone camera and can't take his eyes off it. Immediately, he looks for his mom—scanning the venue for women wearing magenta-coloured dresses and sees her in less than a minute.

'Mom, you have to buy me that flying machine tomorrow.'

Reeti knows Lakshya doesn't like blunt refusals and that he is best tackled by misleading him. As a young boy, Lakshya was told of the imaginary baba who picked up children, packed them in a gunny bag and took them away to make them beg—this played a vital role in the kid's upbringing, especially when he needed to be put to sleep. But, by the age of four years, Lakshya had discovered the hoax.

Reeti says with a straight face, 'The government has given orders that this machine is not to be operated by persons below eighteen years. The police are likely to catch you using it.'

Surprisingly, Lakshya agrees with his mom without an argument. He has just sighted his friends and has run to join them. They move towards the open ground alongside the seating area and start chasing each other.

Once exhausted, they decide to take a food break.

Lakshya bumps into Vanya, who proudly introduces her

cute brother to her friends, some of whom are meeting him for the first time.

'How adorable,' Akriti says as she caresses Lakshya's rosogolla-like cheeks.

Lakshya isn't smiling; he has dealt with enough petting over the years, now that he is older, he feels that it is a violation.

'Do you have a boyfriend?' Lakshya asks Akriti, surprising her.

'Yes, as cute as you,' she smiles.

Another girl, Shonali, asks Lakshya, 'Whom do you love the most: mom, papa, Vanya, dada or dadi?'

'None of the above,' Lakshya replies.

'Then, who is it?' Vanya is curious. She presumes that he will astound them by announcing his crush on some girl in the colony.

'My favourite is Miss Sia, the English madam at school. Unlike mommy, papa and others in the house, she never scolds me and also calls me sweetheart. One day I am going to marry her!' Lakshya beams.

Vanya's face gets flushed. 'This is outrageous.'

'It is okay. Outspoken kids turn out to be more successful in life than the quiet ones,' Shonali opines.

13

The Nostalgia Club

Kimti has an itch; he wants to head towards his drinking buddies.

Soon, Salwinder Singh, his friend, who *always* wears a maroon turban, recognizes Kimti from a distance, because of Kimti's henna-dyed-orange hair. Kimti would love to sport jet black hair but he is allergic to the dye, just as much as he is allergic to teetotallers, Tripta's brother, Reeti's friends and Kushal's green ideas.

He joins his buddies who are sitting around the table near the drinks station, which is to be the nucleus of their existence tonight. Salwinder is wearing a safari suit, a style that is on the verge of extinction, alongside home-knitted woollens, pleated trousers, submissive wives and courtesies. Although most of them need to carry a walking stick, they avoid it in public, especially at parties. Kimti reaches out and moves the flower vase from the table and puts it on the ground, beneath the table; it is obstructing his view of his friends.

Darshan Lal, the man with the pencil moustache, asks Kimti the typical question, 'How is your health?'

Kimti grins. 'Suffice to say that whenever my wife wakes up at night, she looks at me to check if I am breathing! It seems she wants to breathe easy by living some years without me.'

Salwinder raises his brows. 'Why are you making fun of Tripta bhabhi? She takes such good care of you. Any other lady would have left a rascal like you long ago!'

'You may be right. I am a redundant entity in the house. How times have changed. When I was a handsome and successful young man, I was a terror for my in-laws because I invariably threw around my pride while attending marriages. Back then, my brother-in-law was deputed to be constantly by my side. He literally waited on me! But, over the last few years, the tables have turned and how! If I try to repeat my tantrums, I am likely to be kicked out of the venue by a rapid-response team comprising my brother-in-law and my wife,' Kimti says sorrowfully.

Darshan seems to agree with him. 'Yes, a lot has changed. In our times, an entire family of a close relative would threaten to boycott the wedding ceremony because of real or imaginary insults. Once, my elder brother had to take off his turban and lay it at the foot of a khadoos elder to defuse a volatile situation.'

Kimti continues, 'Nowadays arranging a wedding ceremony is as easy as saying "one two three". It is tougher to coax the youngsters into wedlock; many of them just want to have a live-in relationship forever! And with this multitude of wedding services providers, there is no need to coax an army of relatives and friends to be honorary workers and managers. Tripta and I were married in a community hall where faded tents were put up by a tent provider, where huge pedestal fans fanned hot air at us and stray dogs were among the guests. The old waiters wore uniforms riddled with repair patches, and they served with a frown. The teetotallers among the family were assigned the most boring job—to oversee the distribution of drinks. Afterwards, some guests felt sick from overeating while others went down with food poisoning.'

'But there was one good thing about that era: the marriages provided a safe zone for the boys and girls to steal glances at each other and many love stories were seeded—including mine! Nowadays, the marriage ceremony seems to have lost its sanctity. Look at the divorce rates,' Salwinder says. As he speaks, his neck rotates. It is a gradual process that allows the visual axis of his eyeballs to align constantly with the changing position of a noteworthy guest of the fairer sex.

'Leave alone the live-in relationships, even extra-marital affairs are commonplace,' Kimti adds. He feels like telling them that infidelity is going on right under his nose, but then his mind applies emergency brakes on his vocal apparatus.

'Chalo, enough nostalgia,' Darshan says. 'Let us talk about the present. An old age home with five-star facilities has opened somewhere on the outskirts of Ludhiana. So we can threaten our family members that we may run away from home if they try to give us the impression that we are a nobody.'

Kimti's eyes gleam. 'I am ready to move there right away. Just a few of you have to accompany me!' They laugh and after a while, Kimti gestures, 'It is time to clink glasses,' and the others share high amplitude nods.

They move towards the drinks counter where pretty female bartenders smile at them. There are innumerable options on display, including wines, tequila, beer and gin but Kimti understands only blended scotch whisky.

'Sohneyo, one 60 ml peg please! Add some soda, some water and two cubes of ice.' He points out his brand to the bartender, who returns his compliment with a measured smile before picking up the peg measure.

While looking at the youngsters who are getting their drinks mixed, Kimti is reminded of his own youth. Since his father followed a 'purely stick policy, sans the carrots', he had to consume alcohol on the sly at home. He would pour his liquor into a stainless-steel glass and would gulp it down at the most unusual bar—the bathroom of his house. All the while, his parents thought that their son took a long time to bathe because he was obsessive about hygiene.

Soon, everyone is back at their table.

Kimti passes a two hundred rupee note to a waiter. 'Beta, snack service should be A-one.'

'Jee, sahib,' replies the waiter, whose body language has changed soon after the tip.

Suddenly, Salwinder gets up from his chair. 'This is the right time to make an important announcement, right before we get high on these drinks. Everyone is invited to attend the marriage of my granddaughter; it is just three months away. Proper invitations will reach you later.'

Kimti pouts his lower lip, 'I will surely come, if I manage to stay alive till then.'

Salwinder looks unblinkingly at Kimti. 'Never say things like that. We can't imagine life without you.'

Kimti becomes moist eyed. 'Really. I never knew I was so valued.'

'It is generally agreed that there has been only one great personality who has hailed from Ludhiana—apart from Sahir Ludhianvi Sahib—and that is Kimti Lal,' Salwinder says. Then, he starts laughing. His laughter appears in bursts, similar to the sound of the engine of a four-stroke motorcycle. The others laugh even louder, only to reveal that visits to their dentist were overdue.

Kimti's lips start to quiver. 'I got it. You decaying oldies have decided to have fun at my expense. I wish and pray that all of you are born as dogs in your next incarnation.'

'Please be more specific. Street dogs or pet dogs? Pet dogs get lots of kisses and cuddles from pretty ladies,' Salwinder laughs.

Their conversation is interrupted as they are joined by Faqir Sain, who receives many sympathetic glances. It is rumoured that a few days before Diwali he gambled in an inebriated state, put his factory on stake—and then, he lost it.

Faqir Sain greets everyone and then speaks, 'Before you ask anything, let me clarify. Whatever you have heard is absolutely true! But I have learnt my lesson. Gambling and drinking should never be combined; they should be enjoyed separately! Or else, a wealthy man may become a faqir!'

Kimti furrows his brows. 'So you are still not ready to leave your gambling days behind?'

'No, I have to win back my factory.'

Kimti folds his hands. 'Jai ho. I have seen many freaks in my life but you are peerless. However, you are carrying forward the legacy of the kauravas and the pandavas.'

The attention of the group is attracted by a man standing nearby, who has dared to wear a simple kurta and dhoti at a marriage in Ludhiana.

Faqir Sain reveals, 'He is Ramalingam, a close business associate of Narinder. Mind you, he is so rich that he can take all our businesses! But, as you can see, he does not smell of money.'

Kimti replies, 'Our DNA is different. If we earn, say, a sum of five lakh per month, we have a lifestyle worth ten lakhs.'

The Tamilian recognizes Faqir Sain and shakes hands with him. He is offered a seat at the table and joins the group. Ludhianvis are in awe of South Indians and assume that all of them have an IQ equivalent to that of Ramanujam.

'So, are you having a good time at the party?' Kimti asks.

'Yes. Today, like everyone else, I too want to imagine that I am a mayfly,' Ramalingam quips. The vacant look on everyone's faces makes it clear to Ramalingam that the reference went over their head.

Faqir Sain thinks, *'Ramalingam could use even more complex language; he can make all of us appear unpolished.'* He tries to steer the conversation into a safe zone. 'Have you eaten anything?'

'Nothing much according to your standards!' Ramalingam

says with a wry smile. 'Actually, I had my fill having sampled various snacks. You Punjabis have begun to spoil the other Indian communities! They are now so influenced by your "shaking a leg, high on a peg" lifestyle that quite a few of them have started aping it.'

'All that leads to more consumption—which is good news for the Indian economy,' Darshan says.

14

Men of Spirits

For quite some time, Reeti has been quiet. She also seems to be staring at Kushal, a 'get out of my sight' type of look. People-watching has provided Kushal with some succour. At every wedding, he has been surprised, having come across old classmates, old neighbours, old flames and even old enemies.

He tries to have the safest conversation he can think of between husband and wife; he talks about the kids.

'Listen, I am not happy with Vanya's company at the school,' he says.

'Umm...' Reeti offhandedly responds and turns her face away.

'I... will just check out some friends,' he says and walks away rebuffed.

Soon, he comes across a woman who looks so angelic that his neck moves involuntarily towards her direction. To his utter delight, she smiles at him.

'Oh, it is Piya, my schoolmate,' he realizes.

Piya's beauty is certified and quantified; she was a finalist in the Miss India contest long back and has been working in television in Mumbai since then. They hug each other. Straightaway, they start talking about their time at The Holy Child School, specifically their eccentric teachers and naughty classmates.

A suited-booted young man approaches them and says, 'May I join in?'

'A sophisticated intrusion,' Kushal mumbles to himself.

'Piya, take my business card. Give me a missed call on my cell number. From now on, I will be in regular touch with you,' Kushal says and moves on.

Within minutes, he receives a call from Reeti.

'I have been observing you for the last few minutes. How many girlfriends do you have on the sly?' Reeti yells. Her anger resounds and seems to transmitted through the phone.

'Oh! That was Piya, my schoolmate. You haven't met her because she is settled in Mumbai. If you don't believe me, I can make you talk with her.'

'It's okay,' Reeti says and hangs up.

Kushal grumbles, *'If she is going to leave me, why is she bothered about whom I am talking with? I better stay with my male friends. Otherwise Reeti will continue to harbour these delusions about me having multiple partners.'*

He doesn't even try to spot Reeti and moves towards the drinks area; he knows that his friends will gravitate towards it sooner rather than later.

A waiter comes up to him.

'Sir, Hare Bhare Kabab,' he announces.

'Okay,' Kushal takes the paper plate and puts two pieces on it.

'Sir, this is very good. Please have some more.'

Kushal takes a good look at the tall waiter. His face is criss-crossed with wrinkles and he has an affectionate expression.

This chap knows how to serve,' Kushal thinks.

He says, 'What is your name?'

The waiter is left speechless for a moment. Guests rarely ask him for his name or even glance at him for more than a fleeting moment.

'My actual name is Dharmatma, but most people call me Lambu.'

'Where do you come from?'

'I originally belong to East Champaran district in Bihar, but now I call myself a native of Ludhiana—I eat, drink, think and show-off like a Ludhianvi! In fact, I have been staying here since my teenage years. Now, I go back to my village once a year just to make my relatives envious. This city pulsates with dynamism and that keeps me in high spirits.'

'Lambu, how much do you make per celebration?' Kushal can't help asking such an intrusive question.

'What I make here is just a bonus, to feed minor vices like weekend drinks, movies and shopping. I also work during the day in a factory. But being a waiter isn't everyone's cup of tea. If an absent-minded cook spoils a dish by putting excessive salt in it, the guests spoil our mood. If the supplier provides stale paneer, then too we are held responsible. Some of the guests think that kicking our butt forms a part of the party experience!'

Kushal tries to change the topic. 'Okay, tell me about a few interesting incidents you have witnessed at these marriages.'

'I have seen grooms and brides doing the disappearing act or backing off at the last moment, which often leads to arguments among the relatives. Also, the antics of drunks…and so many other incidents. In fact, I can talk for hours on this topic!'

Both of them hear a shout.

'Oye, Lambu!'

A manager wearing a perfectly knotted tie, carrying a walkie talkie set, approaches with hurried steps.

'Sister fucker! Why are you stuck at the same place for so long? The host is complaining about slow service,' the captain bellows.

'Sorry Saab,' Dharmatma says to the manager and moves away, but not before whispering to Kushal, 'See, even our superiors sodomize us whenever they feel like it.'

Kushal tries to hand over a two hundred rupee note to him but Lambu refuses and folds his hands.

'Saab, the respect I have earned from you is priceless.'

Finally, Kushal spots his friend Shanky with a glass of dark yellow whisky in his hands. It seems like he has emptied a full quarter with just a few cubes of ice. *He has gone one up on the Patiala Peg. But this is not uncommon in our city. I think we need a new nomenclature: the Ludhiana Peg.*

Kushal wants to keep it light today. He considers picking up a glass of red wine and sipping on it slowly. Total abstinence is not feasible because if he doesn't consume something alcoholic, his friends will keep pestering him, as if their life hangs on his inebriation.

But he suddenly recalls that he has to get a vodka with fresh lime for Reeti. It has the potential to reverse the direction her mind has taken. He asks the bartender to quickly serve him.

Since it is comparatively early by Ludhiana standards, the venue isn't choc-a-bloc with guests. He locates Reeti easily without any nosy lady by her side.

Reeti accepts the glass but the manner in which she says 'thank you' feels like 'screw you' to Kushal.

Kushal gets his glass of red wine and goes back to his gang, which has now begun to gradually swell to actual numbers.

'What is wrong with you? Only women drink red wine,' mocks Shanky. Except for his palms, Shanky has hair everywhere. He even has hair growing out of his ears. Shanky's real name is Prakhar. In fact, most of Kushal's friends are known by their childhood names—like Bunty, Kaka, Pappu, Bholu, etc., despite their best efforts to persuade others to call them by a proper title. A hefty man, otherwise named Param, continues to be known as 'Nikku' (small boy) while Yudhishther, who is a now a grandfather, is still called, 'Baby'.

To prevent such a situation from becoming legacy, these guys have insisted on a single name for their kids.

Shanky is a jolly fellow who doesn't mind being the butt of many jokes. But he loses his cool when his kids blame him for their own hairiness, ignoring the fact that they have also inherited many good genes from him.

Kushal pleads for his red wine. 'See, I often undertake business trips in countries where wine is commonly drunk. I have developed a taste for it. It is good for the heart too.'

'What is the name of this wine?' Shanky says with a wry smile, almost hoping that Kushal fails this facade.

'This is burgundy, which, as its name suggests, is made in the Burgundy region situated in the east-central part of France. It is made from Pinot Noir grapes. Do you want to know about the wine making process in detail?'

Shanky bends down to touch Kushal's knees. 'Oye yaara. A person as sophisticated as you shouldn't be seen in public with desi people like us. In fact, you shouldn't have settled in Ludhiana at all.'

When two men meet in Ludhiana, the conversation usually begins with, '*Kamm kar kis taran hai?* How is your work, profession or business going on?' This basically implies—are you earning a decent sum of money or have you had to resort to staying at your relatives' homes while on business trips.

Kushal asks the same question to Gundeep Singh who has just joined them.

'Man. One recession follows another in this industry,' Gundeep replies gruffly.

Kushal chuckles, 'Saleya! If you are buying a new Mercedes every year during the recession, God knows what you will do when you do well!'

Predictably, the conversation shifts towards property. This is a topic that never fails to excite Ludhianvis. If you ask a doctor in Ludhiana, 'What is your specialization?' he might reply, 'I am a heart surgeon but I also dabble in property.' Similar statement can be heard from a banker, a researcher and even from a holy man.

Guri, a colonizer of real estate, has arrived after attending another marriage. His eyes are red, a sign that alcohol is already enjoying a luxuriant swim in his bloodstream. The only situation in which Guri doesn't pitch his colony is when he is attending a funeral. Kushal knows he doesn't have all the approvals to do so. What's more, he has been known to sell a plot to two parties simultaneously, by forging the documents. During their last meeting, he had told Kushal, 'I expect you to purchase at least two plots in my colony.' The thought that crossed Kushal's mind at that moment was: *'Even a demon spares those who are close to him.'* He usually evades Guri by citing the many losses at his factory.

'Whenever I am drunk, I never lie!' Guri is at it again, trying to cash in on the universal weakness—trying to find a tree on which money grows. He continues, 'The plots in the Blue-Rose colony are going to appreciate two times in a period of three years! So, don't miss the opportunity because you will repent it later on. The clock is not going to turn back.'

'Liar, Liar. It is now obvious that alcohol is not a truth-telling drug!' Kushal feels.

Suddenly, he sees Lakshya running towards him. 'What is he up to now?'

To his relief, Lakshya hugs him.

Lakshya speaks loudly so that no one misses his complaint.

'Dad, will you keep drinking sharaab all the time or do something else too?'

Everyone smiles. Kushal remembers that when Lakshya was in pre-school, he often used to enquire about the golden liquid

Kushal used to drink at parties. Kushal would reply that he drank a bitter medicine. But a year ago, at a marriage party, Lakshya was adamant on having a second course of pizza. When he was curbed by Kushal, Lakshya had said promptly, 'Dad, get me a pizza or else I will drink a peg of whisky!'

'What is your mom doing,' Kushal asks Lakshya, steering the conversation elsewhere.

'I haven't seen her for a while. You are supposed to keep an eye on her, not me!'

Then, he runs away.

'Your son is so cute,' Gundeep says.

'Cute, but unmanageable. You can exchange your kid with him if you want!'

15

Being a Hostess is No Joke

Reeti locates Kaajal, the bride's mother, to greet her in person and also to part with the shagun amount before she forgets. She notices Kaajal, and that she has deliberately placed her left hand in a manner that occasions glimpses of her diamond ring. As Reeti tries to hand over the envelope, Kaajal moves her hands away. 'There was no need for this,' she says.

Reeti is aware that it is a convention to not accept the shagun amount without putting up a token resistance. She tries again, 'This is a small token of appreciation.'

This time, Kaajal holds the envelope and puts it into her Prada handbag. Later, a thorough evaluation will be conducted, outlining who gave how much. Although no one keeps a written record, the hosts miraculously remember the amount gifted by others; in the future, everyone has to be paid back in the same coin.

While Kaajal is enjoying the steady stream of true and

false compliments of her guests, a part of her is steeped in melancholy because after tonight, Nancy, the livewire of her house, will depart to her new home. She is also worried that her pampered daughter's paucity of life skills could lead to a comedy of errors on a daily basis while juggling the various roles and responsibilities within her new family.

To add to her woes, eunuchs and street singers have been making a beeline to her house. She is cocksure that they are making use of social media to spread the news that a moneyed family's marriage celebrations are on. While her bargaining skills have helped her ward off most of them with minor amounts, the eunuchs have extorted considerable cash using their time-tested tactic of threatening to disrobe publicly; this works much like pointing a loaded revolver at someone's temple.

In fact, for the last six months, she hasn't even had the time to scratch her head, what with all the wedding shopping and other preparations. Whenever she has asked her daughter to go on her own, Nancy insisted that Kaajal accompany her because of her ability to squeeze an extra bargain. Nancy especially loves her mother's theatrics during the haggling process, particularly her cynical high-pitched laugh.

Kaajal knows to then say to the salesman, 'This is daylight robbery! The price that you are quoting is double that at the other shops.' The senior-most salesman in the shop, on hearing this, would take over and it invariably ends with him too being left on the verge of tears.

Sometimes, Kaajal's friends ask her why she bargains to such an extent, despite being so rich. Kaajal has a standard reply—'we have become rich because of the bargaining we have done while conducting business and while shopping!'

During the shopping expeditions, the to-be bride was made to apply a thick layer of sunscreen; life-giving sun labelled as a tan-inducing villain. A course of fairness inducing Glutathione injections were also taken from a fairly famous cosmetology clinic to ensure fair amounts of compliments from the 'fairness fixated' guests.

Nancy has even gone to the extent of eating only boiled vegetables just to carry off the mehnga-lehnga which will show quite a bit of her tummy. When she was not shopping, she was either bugging her dietician or dancing to the tunes of Zumba. In addition, she took yoga classes from a lady who is a disciple of a jet-setting swami. The strategy was similar to carpet bombing—try to hit everything everywhere and something will be on target. But the victory has been symbolic; she managed to lose just three kilos.

'It is not going to be over today. The reception is tomorrow. Thankfully, the groom's family is responsible for the arrangements. I will drink to my heart's content and dance like crazy,' Kaajal thinks.

She is expecting that the newly-weds will also find some respite from putting on plastic smiles for the myriad of guests and visitors after they leave for their honeymoon. They plan to visit a Greek Island, whose name she hasn't been able to pronounce properly. After that, invitations to the couple have already been determined; a line of close relatives and friends have planned bashes at their homes. In Ludhiana, the newly-weds are properly introduced to a family only after many proper dinners, during which calorie counting is a cognizable offence. Kaajal is worried about her daughter's dresses becoming undersized because of the overzealous hosts who take the guests hostage and then take control over the serving spoons. Requests of 'no more please' are brushed aside by saying:

'Just a bit more.'

'You have hardly had anything.'

'This is our family's speciality. You have to taste it.'

'Don't feel shy beta. This is your own house.'

'You won't become fatter after just one good meal.'

'To compensate for this, you can do a vigorous workout tomorrow.'

'You have to eat this. I have made it with my own hands.'

Some girls give in because they don't want to give the impression of being a snob. Of course, some dishes are so tempting that the young brides can't help but treat their self-control with the snub it deserves.

Kaajal's eldest daughter was married at a destination wedding in Goa. But the guests from Ludhiana maintained their reputation of causing mayhem whenever they visit a resort as marriage guests. As usual, the primary cause of friction with the management of the resort was due to their policy of a fixed timing for drinks. Also, many relatives and friends, who thought they were worthy enough to be invited to Goa, but were not in the guest list, later showed their displeasure in subtle and not so subtle ways. Kaajal is well aware that grudges about being ignored for a marriage invitation can be passed from generation to generation.

So, the Kumars dropped their original idea of celebrating this marriage as a destination wedding on a cruise ship and decided to have it in Ludhiana itself, where there is no dearth of venues to spend an obscene amount of money for a single evening of celebration.

Kaajal expects everyone to sing praises about the event and if someone doesn't do so, she extracts an eulogy, asking, 'What do you think about the venue and the arrangements?'

But she has a different question for Reeti, 'How do I look?'

'Useless question. Nobody would reply that you are looking bad. But even her expensive chiffon saree and diamond necklaces are unable to compensate for her overdone mascara and excessive rouge,' Reeti smiles to herself.

She stares at her for a while and then says, 'You are looking so fabulous, even ladies who are the age of your daughter may feel jealous.'

Kaajal's eyes have stars. 'Still, I am nothing in comparison to you,' she says, returning the adulation.

A buxom lady with perfect curls, who seems to have come straight from a shopping jaunt in Milan, interrupts them without caring for niceties. She and Kaajal hug each other as if they are long lost friends. The intruder doesn't even look towards Reeti.

Reeti assesses quickly. *'It is better to move away unless I want to experience how it feels when a super-rich woman ignores a reasonably rich woman!'*

As Reeti walks back, she notices men of different sizes, shapes and ages feasting their eyes on her. She is reassured about her wide and strong magnetic field.

Just as she begins to wonder whether Jasmine, her mother, has arrived, Reeti gets a call from her and they quickly find each other.

'My doll looks stunning in whatever she wears,' Jasmine says.

'Thanks mom,' Reeti says, her smile terminating prematurely.

'What is it baby? Apart from your ill-fated dress, you are upset about something else. Nobody can read you like your mom. Come on. Open up.'

'Kushal is cheating on me.'

'What! Unbelievable!'

As Reeti tells her all about how the lid was blown off Kushal's secret affair, Jasmine is all attention. But neither she nor Reeti are shedding tears.

'So, it is an old girlfriend. I don't think any woman from a well-off family in Ludhiana would even give him a lift. Anyway, how do we wean this female off him?' Jasmine wonders.

'Mom, there is no need for that. I have made up my mind. I plan on leaving him for good. You know I have been adjusting with him and his low income for so long. Leave alone a new factory, he hasn't even put up any new units in the factory for the last so many years. And on top of that, he is a cheat.'

'Beta, I leave it to you. Right now, you have a solid reason to leave him if you decide to do so. The doors of our house are always open for you. And there would be no dearth of suitors for you after this should you break off the marriage with such a loser.'

'All this is between you and me. At least for tonight.'

'Okay.'

Punita, Reeti's best friend, joins them. She looks resplendent in a designer dark green dress with peacock motif. It makes Reeti pine for her missing dress yet again.

Jasmine decides to let them have their private conversation. 'I have a long list of people to meet! I will catch up with you later.'

Punita begins. 'So, what's up?'

Reeti feels like telling Punita all about the unimaginable things that have happened to her all through the day but decides against it—Punita is known to uncork her bottle of secrets soon after imbibing a glass of wine or vodka.

'Life always throws a surprise your way when you least expect them. Isn't it?' Reeti says vaguely instead.

'Disappointment is written all over your face. I know it is because of the dress fiasco. I have scanned the whole venue but didn't find anyone wearing a similar outfit,' Punita says.

Reeti rests her chin on her right palm. 'I could have taken the risk and worn it.'

'But you are still not safe. Guests are still coming in. Of course, you could wear it later, once only the close relatives are left. As they say—something is better than nothing!'

'Oh! I never thought of doing something like that. I haven't brought along the dress either. But I still wouldn't be able to post pictures wearing the special dress.'

'You can skip the pics and just wear the dress. At least there will be some consolation.'

'But how can I get the dress delivered here? Our driver has gone to attend a marriage in his family. I need to find out some other way. Chalo, let us leave this topic for now. I have had just one vodka and I would like more.'

'Me too. I will tell my hubby to get two glasses.'

Soon they are enjoying the unique Indian pairing of vodka with aloo tikki.

Punita asks Reeti, 'How is Kushal doing?'

With alcohol having undone the valve of inhibitions, Reeti comes out with the truth.

Punita's light grey eyes grow wider and wider as she listens to Reeti. 'Why didn't you tell me earlier today? I never hide anything from you. I have even told you about my one-night stand with Vansh, my old class-fellow and that too scene by scene, without any cuts! This means you don't think of me as a best friend.'

'My dear Punita, don't complicate matters. I even hid everything from my mom and only spoke with her a few minutes ago. I really did not want to disrupt this beautiful event.'

'Okay. Explanation accepted. But you have me really worried. My husband also seems like a harmless character but I think I should spy on him by all means possible. However, I would still advise you to give Kushal another chance. He is basically a good person. This just seems like an old affair re-activated. I hope you have not been neglecting him recently. To give you an example, feigning a headache when he wants to make love. Or, being miserly with hugs and kisses.'

'Not at all. Anyway, what he has done is not justified in any circumstances. You know one of the main reasons for marrying a not-so-handsome man was that he would remain devoted to me forever.'

'I leave the decision to you. After all, you are not a dumb girl; you have acted as an agony aunt for so many friends in their hour of need,' Punita concludes.

16

Whiskey-Shiskey

Kushal's gang is now proportionately large. They are joined by Tinka, a balding industrialist, who is drinking single malt whisky diametrically opposite to the way it should be drunk—gulping it down as if it will evaporate.

'I always drink the first peg fast so that I am high within a few minutes,' he defends himself.

The waiters with vegetarian snacks stop coming into this zone as they are brusquely ordered—no ghaasphoos is allowed and only non-vegetarian snacks are welcome here. The Amritsari fish fry has turned out to be the most requested item.

Shanky seems closest to nirvana, judging by the expression he is sporting; 'I don't need anything else in life,' it seems to say. His wife and mother bicker a lot but are united on one issue—both are strict vegetarians and have placed a blanket ban on non-vegetarian items at their house.

Kushal tries his best to create a barrier between himself and his taste buds but once he tastes a piece of his favourite, the tawa mutton tikka, he surrenders to them and fills a plate with the melt-in-the-mouth morsels. The others too are devouring snacks without any 'checks and balances'. The alcohol seems to have converted their stomachs into big sacs, making the other abdominal organs huddle in a corner.

Kushal hears loud conversations and shouting behind his back.

He turns around to find two youth raining blows on each other and simultaneously blurting out the most insulting abuses. Luckily, the crowd around them don't take sides and increase the number of fighters. Instead, they are being held back from causing damage.

'What happened?' Kushal asks Sohan, an acquaintance.

'The guy in the red shirt made a loose comment about a girl little knowing that her boyfriend was overhearing the conversation,' Sohan reveals.

'One can say that the ears of the boyfriend happened to be at the wrong place at the wrong time,' Kushal says in American accented English.

'Kushal, please don't use such complicated language. My head has started to spin,' Sohan walks away.

Most of Kushal's friends are now using cuss words as conjunctions. He knows from experience that sparks can easily fly with even a minor provocation.

Gundeep is about to put a piece of chicken malai tikka into his mouth, but all of a sudden, he stops and focuses his gaze on the tiny black object on the tikka. Then, he shouts at the waiter who is serving it. 'Call your superior. Right now!'.

The waiter, sensing some major trouble brewing, brings the captain in a jiffy.

'Yes, sir,' the captain says as he braces for the verbal assault.

'Sir de bachey. What is this! You are trying to make us eat insects! Look at this dead ant stuck on the chicken tikka,' Gundeep scowls.

The captain examines the tikka. 'Sir, you are worrying unnecessarily. This is just a piece of burnt jeera.' In a flash, the manager takes the piece of chicken tikka and places it in his own mouth, makes rapid chewing movements and swallows it. Having seen another man eating, Gundeep's tense facial muscles relax. 'Okay. I think I may be drinking too fast. Sorry for the trouble.'

Kushal's eagle eyes have already given their report. *'The gallant catering manager has swallowed a dead ant to avoid elephantine trouble for him and for the catering company he is working for.'*

Then, Guri addresses Kushal. 'What's the matter? You are behaving as if GST has been levied on smiling!' He puts on a creepy smile. 'It seems Reeti has caught you in a compromising position with a girlfriend.'

Kushal's eyes widen. *'Guri is only a bit off the mark. Does the whole world already know about me and Diksha? The other possibility is that Guri has acquired mind-reading capabilities. Most likely, and I hope this is true: he has just made an intelligent guess.'*

Guri continues, 'Come on, confess and you will feel lighter. Everything will stay between us.'

Kushal knows that his friends are basically good at heart but when they are tipsy, they can act like the ancient town-criers.

He keeps mum.

'Come on, Guri. Think before you speak. Kushal is the only decent one among us. I have never even heard him make a comment behind the back of a lady. How can he cheat on his wife?' Shanky intervenes.

'Never underestimate Cupid. It has even hijacked the minds of ascetics who have meditated for years in the caves. I am only a small fry,' Kushal feels like telling Shanky.

A lie is his only option. 'Actually, there are some issues at the factory that are weighing on my mind.'

However, the discussion has him thinking. *'Once Reeti leaves me taking the kids with her, I will have no choice but to travel solo throughout the journey of my life. Diksha is not going to take the extreme step of leaving her family for me; she is far more practical than I am. It is quite unlikely that a lady from Ludhiana would be interested in someone who has been driving the same car for years and years. Also, I don't have the looks to hook anyone. I am doomed!'*

Then, a bulb lights up in his head. He has recently read in a self-help book that mediation can even solve intractable conflicts, provided the mediator is respected by both parties. There is no better person for this than Jasmine, his mother-in-law.

'I need to go to the loo. Will join you guys soon,' he tells his friends quickly and starts looking for Jasmine.

She is in front of the papdi chaat stall, along with two other women. They seem to be deeply focused on the vital task at hand—deciding on the sequence in which the different components of the chaat are to be picked with the spoon to introduce into the mouth.

He calls her. 'Mummy ji, I have an important issue to discuss with you. Please come to the centre of the venue. I'm standing near the elevated picture booth.'

'I know what you are going to talk about. I will be there, but only once I have finished this divine papdi chaat. I have seen lots of ups and downs in my life but I have never compromised on living a good life!'

Kushal has mixed feelings. *'Reeti was not supposed to reveal everything to her mom so soon. She has broken her promise... but, of course, this pales in comparison to my treachery!'*

Jasmine reaches the booth in a few minutes. Kushal puts on an apologetic face and keeps his gaze downcast for an added effect.

'Mummy ji, I am so ashamed of myself that I feel like running away to the hills and becoming a sanyasi.'

'Stop this dramebaazi! I have said nothing all these years despite you depriving my daughter of even the most basic of necessities because I presumed you were at least faithful to her. Tell me, have you gifted her anything decent in all these years? My girl is one in a million and still she is living in such penury. I personally have had to buy clothes and jewellery for her. And on some occasions, I had to get clothes for Vanya and Lakshya too!' Jasmine says.

'I promise you that I will undergo such a transformation that you won't believe it is the same Kushal. I will concentrate solely on my industry and also get cosmetic surgery done. Please help me save my marriage. I have already given word to Reeti that I will never contact that woman again.'

'Reeti used to have her way when she was unmarried! I think she is even more independent now. So she herself will decide what to do. Anyway, she is still young and attractive and will be able to find a man who is a hundred times better than you!'

'I don't deny that! But, please. Try to convince her to give me one chance.'

'I will think about it.' Jasmine gives him a derisive stare and leaves him standing.

He joins his friends. By now, many of them have acquired a slurred accent.

When Shanky's body starts to wobble where he is standing, he knows it is time to put the brakes on. 'I am done with the drinks,' he says at the top of his voice.

This demand isn't digested by anyone in the group except for Kushal. There are multiple voices directed at him, each taking the tone of a beggar.

'Please, have one more—just keep me company.'

'One last peg, lovely lovely.'

'Don't leave this. Let us not waste things.'

'You've hardly had any whisky.'

Suddenly, a man appears out of nowhere.

'Meet my enemy number one! My brother-in-law,' Shanky says. Ever since Shanky injured himself at a party three months ago after a fall following 'one drink too many', his wife follows the adage—prevention is better than cure. But she is a pragmatic person and doesn't expect him to stop drinking completely.

'Sorry for the interruption,' says Vikram, who has been deputed by Shanky's wife to whisk him away from the red zone.

17

Make Room for the Groom

Reeti's cousin, nicknamed Raunki, approaches Kushal and gives him a nudge. 'Chalo, chalo, the marriage procession has finally arrived.'

As a close relative, Kushal has no choice but to be at the forefront of the group receiving the groom and his entourage. Although they are late by two and a half hours, the baraatis don't seem to be in a hurry to enter the venue. They linger at the entrance, dancing to the beats of a dhol and in the process, test the patience and the knee joints of the hosts. Although the traditional brass band comprises old men with sunken cheeks and bored stares, they are playing the latest tunes.

The highway is partially blocked, creating yet another minor bottleneck. But the vehicle drivers slow down without hurling abuses because they behave the same way whenever they are part of a marriage procession.

The groom is sitting atop a chariot; the earlier white mare that accompanied the groom is increasingly being given a pass because the modern groom can easily get a sore bottom from the saddle. As if they aren't already loud enough, the baraatis have also arranged for fireworks.

The dancing appears to be spontaneous but some of the revellers, including the geriatrics, seem to be dancing with exaggerated movements—probably to display their own virility and vitality. The fact that many of them are receiving Mercedes cars as gifts from the bride's family also adds to their verve. Of course, it is a given that most of them have been drinking since the afternoon or even the morning. If the cars accompanying the marriage procession were to be searched, most of them would have a bottle or two of whisky in the boot.

Finally begins the milni ceremony, wherein the close relatives from the bride and the groom's side exchange hugs and garlands one by one, signifying that it is a marriage of two families. Many are coveting the business affiliations this will conceive.

Mismatch ensues between the two maternal uncles, a la Laurel and Hardy—the heavier one playfully lifts the lighter one.

Before being allowed in, the groom has to cut the ribbon. On the opposite side, the bride's cousins and friends have gathered expectantly to extort him, a practice which is condoned by the law as well as society. A lot of banter is exchanged wherein the bride's team has the upper hand. The initial demand is for three lakh rupees, but after a sustained period of haggling, the deal is settled for one lakh only. Kushal is not too enthused by this as he has already seen this orchestrated drama unfold so many times.

The baraatis move inside. The waiters rush towards them with food and drinks as if they are going to break their fast unto death. The groom is surrounded by male cousins and friends who are leering at the pretty girls, hoping to meet their eyes and catch their fancy.

Kushal spots Manjinder, a journalist.

'Hey, what are you doing here? Smelling a rat?' Kushal chuckles.

'Ha ha. For a change, I am not looking for a story. Just covering the marriage. We are going to feature it in the lifestyle section of our newspaper.'

'So, you want to stimulate others to have even fatter weddings. You should instead write an article headlined: "Marriages in Ludhiana—What a Waste of Money!"'

'If you hate Ludhiana so much why don't you live as a nomad in Ladakh? Rear a few Yaks. They will give you everything—food, transportation and material for making clothes and tents.'

Kushal grins. 'The way I am screwing up my personal life and my business, I will have no choice but to do something like that pretty soon!'

An acquaintance waves at Manjinder. He and Kushal say goodbye to each other.

Things are firing up on the dance floor. The DJ is playing Punjabi dance numbers, along with music videos on a big screen. The songs portray a set theme: booze, guns, valour, Canada, hot cars and hotter girls.

'No wonder, the younger Punjabis are neck deep materialists,' Kushal philosophizes.

A few dhol players provide an extra bass and enhance the zing of these songs. A few hybrid, indeterminate dance forms can be seen on the stage—a chap is doing the naagin dance inspired from a YouTube video, a few couples are trying to do the salsa and the tango but with less than modest success. The dance floor comes alive when an NRI woman, a model dressed in a mini, shows off some western moves. Scores of men fall in one-sided love at first sight.

Reeti is also watching the show. She is jealous of those who dance so well wearing pencil heels. *'Have they worn heels since they were toddlers?'* she wonders.

Kushal, standing some distance away from Reeti, is talking to Umang, his business associate. 'Women are showing a lot of spirit on the dance floor today… although many of them haven't imbibed any spirit at all,' he jokes.

Umang's friend comes and grabs Umang by the hand, hoping to drag him to the dance floor. Fifteen minutes ago, Umang had sent them back reasoning that he wasn't drunk enough.

But once he reaches the glittering floor, Umang compensates with a belly dance, heaving an imaginary bosom and even performing suggestive gestures with his eyes, making everyone laugh. Thankfully, he doesn't bare his hairy belly.

After he gets tired, Umang starts moving to different parts to find the introverts and bring them to the dance floor. While some refuse to budge, pointing to their knees, others go to the stage and dance with gusto, as if they had been waiting for someone to browbeat their inhibitions all along.

The dance music stops abruptly as the bride enters with a grand procession trailing behind her and an intricately decorated cloth held over her head by her brother and cousins.

Conversations take a break as everyone's dilated pupils turn towards the bride. A wave of jaw dropping follows. The bride's beauty is complemented by her sepia lehnga, which is encrusted with crystals and precious stones. The conversations resume soon with most of the women guessing the price and designer of the lehnga. This detail has been kept secret by the bride's family.

Nancy, the bride, stops on the way, and moves towards the D.J.'s station, surprising everyone. A mike is handed over to her. She sings 'Main Tainu Samjahawan ki,' while looking unwaveringly at the groom. Shobhan, the bridegroom, goes into a trance—this is a surprise for him.

After the song finishes, the couple ascend the stage. But when he tries to garland her, she playfully moves her head back and nods in the negative. The folding of his hands is enough to make her tilt her head forwards. Then both of them are seated on the throne-like couch against a background of a wall of flowers. Instead of coy glances to each other, the couple are chatting animatedly. And why should they not? They have known each other for the last two years, and that too intimately—literally, as well as figuratively.

Kimti looks at them and goes back in time to his marriage. When he and Tripta were in the car just after the Doli, just brushing against her would electrify his whole body.

The music starts again but this time, a lovely, lively compere ascends the stage and invites the couples related to the bride. Although they have held multiple rehearsals under the watchful eyes of the choreographer, many of them are letting her down by incorporating chaotic elements into their dance steps.

Then, the bride ascends the stage to thunderous applause and sings a Punjabi folk song, where she playfully expresses her inability to leave her parental home and go to a new one. After the song ends, the bride and the bridegroom get into the groove, dancing to the tunes of Bollywood songs. Kimti showers bank notes of hundred rupees above their head and tries to join in the dancing. But he wobbles after taking a few drunken steps. Kushal has been observing his antics with a mixture of amusement and annoyance. He supports his father just in the nick of time.

'Dad, you have danced innumerable times in marriages over the years. It is high time you enjoyed this as a spectator. Also, we are not so rich that money can be showered like this!' he grumbles.

Kushal hands over his dad to the geriatric gang.

While returning to the dance stage to watch the rest of the performances, Kushal finds Drish, his relative, slouched on a chair with his eyes closed. It seems that he has had one drink too many. Kushal notices that Drish is breathing, albeit very slowly. *'He is okay but let me contact his brother so that he can be with him.'*

Kushal is able to locate Naman, Drish's brother, after some effort, but the brother too seems to be on the verge of passing out. Without even the slightest sign of worry on his face, Naman says, 'Let him lie there peacefully for a while and he will spring back to life! This is routine. I will surely take him along while leaving.'

By this time, most of the guests have arrived at the venue.

Their sharp minds are estimating the total number of guests at the venue, which is an important parameter for evaluating the grandness of the celebration.

18

Everyone Loves Gossip

Kushal decides to go back to his friends to enjoy their hyperemotional conversations. On the way, he bumps into Rattan Lal, his dad's younger brother. He used to pamper Kushal with chocolates, candies and hugs when Kushal was just a kid. But there was a flip side to this affection: Kushal developed cavities in a few of his teeth and he learnt at a young age that drills find use in one's mouth too.

'Namaste, chacha ji,' Kushal greets him and stoops as low as possible to touch his feet.

But Rattan Lal gives him a cold stare. 'I am ashamed of being your chacha because you have let me down and brought down our illustrious and decent family! I am left wondering what made you cheat on a wife who is so gorgeous.'

Kushal feels the earth move beneath his feet.

'Chacha ji, it seems there is some misunderstanding,' he manages to say.

'You have played on my lap as a child so I know you well

enough. I can easily make out your bluff. Anyway, your dad has told me everything; although, I suspect that he has added some fictional elements to the facts. See, every married man or woman feels like having some variety. That is precisely the reason why societal norms have been made—to keep harmful but natural urges in check. Back in the day, one could get away with such things but nowadays women don't hesitate to kick the man's butt and find a better alternative!'

Realizing that denial is not an option, Kushal says, with downcast eyes, 'Chacha ji, I am sorry. It was my mistake. I promise that I will never repeat it again. But please, keep everything to yourself.'

'What is the use of me keeping it hidden when it is already an open secret? When your father was narrating this story, ten others were listening in, and they were even more attentive than your old studious classmates! And maybe, by mistake, I have already spoken about this with many others. How has Reeti reacted to this?'

'Obviously, she is outraged and is quite likely to announce her farewell soon. Which woman would want to share the affections of her husband with another woman?'

'Never lose hope. Miracles do happen!'

Kushal excuses himself. The veins on his forehead are throbbing; the first thing he wants to do is to confront his father. He moves ahead and finds Kimti in animated conversation with his friends.

'Just a second, Dad,' gestures Kushal.

Kimti gets up and they move away to the side.

'Daddy ji, why are you hell-bent on ruining my life? Where was the need to talk about Diksha to Chacha ji, and that too in front of others?' Kushal says, in a not-too-respectful tone.

'Actually, it is you who is spoiling the reputation of our reputed family!' Kimti says.

'But why are you trying to make this detail viral?'

'I thought things went viral only on social media! My younger brother asked me about your haal-chaal. So, I told him in as many words. "Kushal's haal is okay but chaal-chalan is disturbed." Then he asked me to elaborate on that. So it is his fault!'

'Dad, please. If someone talks about the topic, tell him that you just said all that in a drunken stupor.'

'Anything for you, my puttar!'

However, Kushal is aware that it is too late to control the transmission of such a contagious revelation. It is so saucy that the listener feels that it is his or her moral duty to deliver it to gossip-starved ears and provide much awaited relief.

As he walks away from his dad, Kushal thinks on his feet. *'If I move away from this venue for two hours or so, most of the guests will be gone. So, whatever people say, it will be behind my back and at least, I will not be ridiculed in public.'*

Then his phone pings.

It is an unknown number, but he picks it up only to regret it.

On the line is Reeti's relative, Anika, the firebrand feminist, who has spread as much terror amongst the men of Ludhiana as the man-eating tigress of Kumaon had once spread in present-day Uttarakhand. But there is no Jim Corbett-like character in Ludhiana to help Kushal deal with Anika.

Anika shouts with such an intensity that he has to move the mobile phone away from his ear to protect his eardrums. 'What the hell do you think you are doing? Women have decided that enough is enough—we will make unfaithful men rue their actions. By the way, where are you? I have been searching for you for the last five minutes.'

Kushal cuts the call. The fight-flight-fright response has been activated. He reconsiders: *'It seems I am the topic of conversation among most of the guests at this venue right now. Apart from suicide, the only other option for me is to get out of here immediately. Otherwise, Anika and her cronies are definitely going to beat me with their sandals. And, if some of them have pencil heels on, I have had it. The media in the venue will get a story on a platter. Plus, the impromptu reporters from among the public will record the assault on their smartphones and then forward it to ensure my national and international infamy.'*

As he starts moving towards the front entrance, Kushal feels a hard thump on his back. '*Oh my God! She's got me,*' he trembles.

His suspended breathing resumes after he hears a male voice. 'Oye, Kushal, where are you going? It has been long since we last met.'

Kushal turns around and finds Romy, his bosom pal, who reveals he has just returned from his son's house in Toronto, Canada, prematurely because of 'adjustment problems' with his daughter-in-law, a scenario that Kushal had already predicted and anticipated.

'Tonight, we are going to get dead drunk!' Romy says, his eyes twinkling.

Just as he is contemplating his next move, Kushal's worst fears come true. He observes his gang of friends moving towards him. *'It looks like they have been actively scouting me.'*

They shout in unison, 'Oye! Here comes the great playboy of Ludhiana!'

Tinka bends down to touch his feet and says, 'Gurudev. Please accept me as your pupil! Teach me how to seduce pretty ladies.'

There are other voices adding to the chorus:

'His actual height is double that of what is visible. Rest of his body is underground!'

'Chha gaye, bhaji. It seems "very good" has been inscribed on your manhood!'

'Ah, you must have a girlfriend in every country you visit as an exporter!'

'The difference between our lives and your life is like the difference between an over-the-ground railway and a subway!'

'Tell us your whole story from the beginning, without any cuts!'

Shanky adds, 'Idiots. Instead of making fun of him, try to learn something from him. To impress the ladies, you don't need rippling biceps or tons of money. Wow them with intelligent conversation, just as Kushal does!'

'What does that sound like?' Guri laughs.

'Okay. Let me speak too,' Kushal says with an oblique gaze. 'Whatever you have heard is false. It is but a rumour spread by a person with whom I have a conflict.'

But he sounds unconvincing—just like Bill Clinton when he had stated, 'I didn't have sex with that woman.'

'Excuse me, I just need to talk to Reeti,' Kushal says and he mixes with the crowd and rushes towards the entrance. All the while he stares down at his ill-maintained shoes to avoid eye contact with yet another story monger.

'There is an emergency at home. Get my car! Quick,' Kushal says to the man manning the valet parking counter. His phone pings again, and Shanky's name begins flashing on the screen; he presses on the red icon. *'These rascals want to have more fun at my expense!'*

After his car is on to the highway, Kushal weighs his limited options. *'If I go home, the security guard and the maid will wonder why I have come back without the others. Plus, they are Reeti's lackeys and are certain to call her to give her this information about me.'*

Kushal decides to go to a bar so that he can ruminate over why his luck is below par—over a beer—considering that his friends have been getting away with crimes of passion without being marred by a reputational scar. He knows about a tavern nearby and takes a turn from the highway to reach there. Pieces of semi-cooked kebabs are displayed on skewers within a glass enclosure at the entrance of the Suroor Drinking Place to bait the tipplers.

'My friends and relatives frequent only high-end bars. So, it is safer to go here since no one will recognize me. Also, I am going to leave my blazer in the car. I look like a blue-collar worker anyway,' he thinks.

At the entrance, the two bouncers, whose upper arms are thicker than his thighs, give him a stern look.

In return, Kushal smiles at them. *'These bouncers seem to have lost the ability to use their brains. Do I look like a riotous character?'*

He sits down on a rickety bright red plastic chair. The table is also unstable. Since it is a weekend, the place is full of revellers who believe that a few drinks will purge their bodies of physical fatigue and mental toxicity that has been acquired over the whole working week. Their loud conversation is getting synchronized to create an orchestra of cacophony.

A man, who looks like a hardened criminal, throws the menu and drinks cards on the table. He stares at Kushal, and Kushal interprets it as, *'I have never seen this guy before. Let us get him drunk! Then he will order a lot of food too.'*

Then, Kushal receives Reeti's call. He can't dare to reject it.

She talks more sweetly than he expected her to. 'Where are you? I have been looking for you for quite some time.'

'I have left the venue and taken the car because almost everyone there has come to know about my affair with Diksha—all because of Dad. I have never felt so embarrassed in my life. I went to the Sidhwan Canal to commit suicide but there was no water,' Kushal says, hoping to cash in on the shock value of his words.

'Good joke! I know you even better than you know yourself. You will never commit suicide because you have the environment to take care of. Since your wife and kids are just your sidekicks, it won't matter if they leave you,' Reeti says in the tone of a satirist.

'Come on. I have never felt like that. Family is my base.'

'And you have families in many places! Isn't that so? Okay. Let us come to the point. I want you to come back to the marriage venue soon.'

'There is a major issue. Anika, your cousin, is there. She wants to give me instant punishment for adultery, without any trial.'

'Yes. Anika was with me a short while ago. She was breathing fire and was looking for you. But I have calmed her down with a lie, Kushal. I told her it was just a misunderstanding. Don't cause any further complications now. Let me enjoy my last day as the member of this family! And, don't try to leave early. Narinder will feel bad if you don't attend the marriage rites.'

'Okay… as you say since you have taken care of Anika… but what about the others, especially those who have a loose tongue?'

Reeti speaks after a while, 'I have an idea. I will get one of the rooms attached to the resort opened for you. You can rest there. Also, you will have plenty of time to introspect about why you went astray and lost your loving family. You can come to the venue just before the actual ceremony starts, so as to avoid meeting the formal guests. I have also worked out how to make you reach the room without any trouble. As soon as you reach the venue, I will come outside the gate, near the valet parking, and quickly escort you to that room.'

'What about Vanya? Has she learnt of this?' Kushal says, and awaits her answer with bated breath.

'For once, the generation gap has proved beneficial. She and her friends haven't mixed with the grown-ups. She is unaware that her dad is a playboy!'

Kushal realizes that the conversation is taking a dangerous turn yet again.

'Okay. I am reaching soon,' he says.

'Wait. For all this help you have to do me a minor favour. Go home and get my special dress—I have already shown it to you. You will easily find it in my cupboard. No questions or comments allowed! Simply do what has been told.'

'Okay.'

Reeti ends the call.

Meanwhile, the waiter, who has been patiently waiting for Kushal to finish his call, approaches him. 'Saab, what should I bring? If you haven't decided then I would suggest that you try our tandoori fish. Also, what would you like to drink?'

'Nothing. I am leaving immediately. My grandfather has suffered a heart attack and he has been admitted to Sehat Hospital,' Kushal says and rushes out without waiting for the waiter's reaction.

'What a freakish character. Was he a human or a spirit?' the waiter, who is also a bit tipsy, wonders.

'Sorry Dada ji. I misused your name,' Kushal speaks to the spirit of his deceased grandfather as he gets into his car. On the way, Kushal calls the security guard and the maid to inform them that he is making an unscheduled entry into the house to get something he had forgotten. When he reaches home, he is confronted by sullen faces—they have been denied uninterrupted relaxation.

As soon as he reaches the marriage venue after having picked up the dress, Kushal finds Reeti waiting for him at the entrance. He hands over the dress to her. They move quickly. Kushal keeps his gaze glued to the ground, like a shy bride of the yesteryears.

'How are people reacting? Are there any signs that a mob will form?' he asks Reeti.

'I can see some fingers pointed at you. No guesses as to what they are talking about! But no mob.'

As they move ahead, Kushal hears a familiar voice singing. The instrumentation is as good as the vocals. He looks to his left and stops in his tracks. Bollywood singers, Ramit and Aina, are on the stage along with the music director duo, Karan-Aman. That is not all. Kona and Sharan, the hottest new stars of Bollywood, are dancing with gusto along with their troupe. Almost all the guests in the venue are looking in the direction of the star-studded stage.

'These guys must have charged an insane amount of money to come to Ludhiana. It seems like Narinder is even wealthier than what he is rumoured to be!' Kushal thinks

He has no choice but to skip the live act of his favourite singers. Reeti dumps him in a spacious room with the instruction that he should feign illness if someone happens to intrude. Kushal tries to take a short nap on the well-made bed but fails to reach even the first stage of sleep. The only way to pass time—apart from wallowing in self-pity—is to check his social media.

Kushal checks his notifications on Facebook and finds himself tagged in a post by Simplicity, the youth environmental movement he has initiated. The group had taken baby steps two years ago, but it hasn't been able to achieve any further milestone.

Today, there seems to be a leap forward. He clicks on the video and is filled with pride similar to that of a father on the success of his offspring. In the main Sarabha Nagar Market, around ten boys and girls of the Simplicity Movement are seen. They are wearing t-shirts paired with ill-fitting pleated trousers—a combination which defies trends, logic and convention. The t-shirts are inscribed with words like 'The Earth begs Your Mercy', 'Humans, Don't be Mean' and 'Earth's Soldiers'. These youngsters practice what they preach: they party just once in a blue moon, eat only at home and even buy recycled garments from flea markets.

Lots of people are paying attention to them because they have never before come across such a protest in Ludhiana, the bastion of consumerism. Some are even asking them for a reason for this display of oddity. The post is full of comments because some trolls have initiated a heated discussion. Kushal checks his WhatsApp folders. The video is circulating in three groups. It surely is going viral.

He receives a call from Sharanpreet Singh, the team leader. 'Sir, your idea worked very well. Today alone, many boys and girls have joined Simplicity. We hope to take it forward from here and create a mass movement, spreading all over the country.'

Kushal pumps his right fist into air. 'Carry on young man. I am with you. We will have a meeting in a few days to chalk out the next plan of action.'

'This is surely the beginning of a revolution. My life is made.

What if I don't have a family. I will dedicate my life to the Simplicity Movement. If God takes away something, he often compensates with something else,' Kushal thinks.

Soon, he gives in to sleep.

19

No Dearth of Freaks

Reeti gets goosebumps when she spots Dr Gayatri, the cosmetic surgeon who has designed or rather redesigned her face, at the venue, moving towards her. The complicating factor is that a few of her friends and relatives are in the vicinity. *'What if she announces that I am one of her "favourite clients", one who never misses an appointment. Am I going to become as infamous as Kushal?'* Reeti shudders.

After exchanging the usual courtesies, the angelic Gayatri looks towards Reeti. 'Lady, your features are so proportionate that you don't even require my treatments. But I can use your face as a reference to plan for other clients!'

Reeti looks at Dr Gayatri in awe. *'What a professional. She locks the secrets of her clients in a Godrej safe!'*

The cosmetic surgeon is an experienced hand and knows that most women, and even the men, want to hide their cosmetic surgeries from all; if it were possible they would lie to God.

Accompanying Dr Gayatri is a woman wearing rings studded

with precious stones on all the fingers of both hands, and three necklaces adorning her long neck. Her make up can be compared to that of a Kathakali dancer.

'Ladies, this is the world famous astrologer—Saubhagya ji,' Dr Gayatri announces.

Reeti curls her lips. *'It is strange that even doctors, who are supposed to have an inclination towards science, can have astrologers as friends.'* But she has heard that many Indian surgeons invoke the names of their revered deity before beginning a surgery or a procedure.

Many ladies already know about Saubhagya. Her husband's failed business has forced her to initiate this 'start-up'. Now he is busy—managing her money and studying the specifications of new car models they buy approximately every six months.

Saubhagya quickly hands over multicoloured visiting cards to everyone in the vicinity.

Reeti is put off by this marketing overkill but she hides it.

'Ladies, I have solutions for any issue in your life—including things related to your career and the marriage of your kids, health, family discords, foreign travel, etc. Also, if you are tormented by the "other woman", I can eject her from your husband's mind forever, just like we remove a weed from a wheat field,' Saubhagya says with a flourish, as if fate is her puppet.

Reeti doesn't take the bait. But Rishika fixes up an appointment with her. Saubhagya moves ahead to bait more clients.

At a nearby stall dishing out sandwiches, Reeti spots Vanya with a boy whom she has never seen before. With his oversized tattoos and spiky hair, he strikes a discordant note. Reeti's maternal and protective instinct come to the fore; she waves to Vanya and moves towards them.

'Hi Mom, this is Taru. We have been in touch on Instagram but are meeting for the first time today.'

Reeti feels like telling her, *'Unfriend him immediately from all channels—social media and in person.'*

But she wants to come across as a liberal parent and fakes a smile. 'What do you do?'

Taru lifts his chin and flicks a tuft of hair off of his forehead. 'I have left my computer sciences engineering course to set up a start-up company in Bengaluru.'

Reeti can't restrain herself. 'But you could have done this after completing your degree. I don't understand why so many life coaches and self-help books emphasize that Bill Gates was a college dropout. This is sending a wrong signal to the youngsters.'

Taru smirks. 'But you will make it big only if you take risks and try something different from the rest of the crowd.'

'Good luck to you,' Reeti says.

She decides not to argue further with him. *'His parents must have tried their best to persuade him to follow a straight path and have failed. I will tackle Vanya later on.'*

When Kushal gets up, the clock on his mobile phone shows that it is half-past midnight. His stomach is rumbling, forcing him to make a dash for the dining hall. There, bleary eyed waiters are waiting to wind off things and he is lucky to find some still-hot food. As a bonus, he finds a group of chronic bachelors comprising men as well as women, all of whom have formed a sort of community, although they haven't formalized it. But that is in the pipeline, they hint.

Kushal is fond of them and wants their tribe to gain in number. *'Fewer marriages will lead to fewer new births and thus, fewer human beings on earth, which will reduce the strain on nature.'*

'Why is it late for you guys?' Kushal asks.

'I, along with my family, had a meeting with the family of a prospective bride. My mother is still hopeful that one day I will bring home her daughter-in-law,' replies Vishal, their ringleader; he has just turned forty-one.

'So, how did you ward them off?' Kushal smiles.

'The girl, along with her family, visited our home. After a while, both of us were told to interact in private. So we went to the terrace. I told her that she should not be impressed by our palatial home. We are under a mountain of debt. After that, she didn't talk much. Her family didn't stay at our home for too long and have never contacted us again.'

'Good. I might join the bachelors' club soon,' Kushal laughs and rushes out of the dining hall into the lawns, leaving his friends to do the guesswork.

The Bollywood troupe has finished its act and the DJ has taken over for the past hour. A group of relatives are still dancing, energized by a cocktail of alcohol, euphoria and a good music system.

The DJ is glancing at his watch every few minutes. Then, he announces, 'Guys and gals! Coming up with the last song. Please dance to your heart's content!'

'No, we want to dance for a little longer,' chants the crowd.

'Sorry. Time's up. My home is far away and I have got to go,' the DJ says politely.

Suddenly, a man takes out a revolver and points it out at the DJ. 'Vajja saaleya,' he shouts.

To everyone's utter surprise, the DJ moves a bit forward and swells his chest. 'Fire the shot. I am not afraid,' he says, clenching his jaws and making a fist.

The man with the revolver freezes, as if he has been caught playing the 'statue game'. The security staff overpower him.

After all the ungodly activities, God is finally invoked as the actual marriage ceremony takes place. Reeti has changed into her dream dress and is getting compliments in wholesale. Some men are straining their eye muscles to look at her from the corner of their eyes while others are more brazen.

The focus soon shifts to the couple as the ceremonies start.

As soon as the seven rounds around the holy fire are completed, there is a frenzy for the newly-wed couple to touch the feet of the elders while the relatives go on a hugging spree.

Vidai, the journey of the bride for her new home, has its usual poignant scenes. The bride breaks down and that precipitates crying amongst the emotionally labile relatives.

Kushal notes that tears are also trickling down Reeti's hazel eyes. *'Reeti must be thinking of the moment when she was a bride.'* He is reminded of the moment when she entered her new home, scattering drops of oil and moving the rice bowl with her foot. How lovely she looked at that moment.

20

Will She Won't She

It is time for Kushal and his family to leave and head back home. Kushal tries to wake Lakshya, who has been sleeping in a guest room.

Lakshya rubs at his eyes. 'Dad, I can't walk. Pick me up.'

'Sure, bachu.'

'I am sorry, my son. I have spoiled your life and that of everyone else in the family,' Kushal murmurs softly.

As he tries to get into the driver's seat, Reeti obstructs him. 'I will drive. You are not in a condition to do so.' Kushal hands over the car key to her.

After they reach home, Kushal and Reeti move to their bedroom. Reeti shuns any eye contact with him.

'I am taking a shower,' she says.

As usual, Reeti takes a long time in the shower, as if she has to sterilize herself.

Kushal rests his chin on his right palm. *'What now? My apologies have fallen flat and emotional blackmail regarding the kids has also come a cropper. What if I get Diksha to talk to Reeti? She can promise her that she will never meet me...'*

Moments later, he bobs his head sideways. *'This is a harebrained scheme. When two competing tigresses meet, a fight is the most probable scenario.'*

He looks up the legalities of divorce on the internet. The lawmakers have purposely made the legal divorce procedure cumbersome so as to make it imperative for the husband or wife to try to live with their differences.

Reeti enters the room in the most unsexy night dress she could have found in her collection.

'Give me one chance, please. Whatever I have done is wrong and there is no justification for it,' Kushal says, although he has little hope of any impact that his cliched words may have.

But his eyes are wide after he hears her sobs. They are followed by a free flow of saline drops. Their eyes meet and the blinking is paused for a while.

When the tears stop, she speaks. 'I confess, I too have cheated on you. It is all because of Facebook. Piyush is an old schoolmate, now settled in Canada. I haven't met him recently but both of us have been chatting for the last few months.'

Kushal gently nudges Reeti's face and lets it rest on his left shoulder.

Reeti continues, 'I lost my balance because he wrote such romantic poems exclusively for me. Actually, he is an accomplished poet and writer.'

Before she can convey any more sordid details, Kushal interrupts. 'He may have sent the so-called exclusive poems to many simultaneously! Anyway, I don't want to know more than what you have told me.'

Reeti's crying resumes. Kushal also joins her as his tear glands finally sense an opportunity to shed their load. He is vulnerable after a long time. It is a scene straight out of a romantic flick—Reeti opens her arms and they hug each other.

Kushal says, 'We are even now! The past is behind us. Let us take a pledge that we will never do this again.'

'I was about to say the same thing,' Reeti replies with a faint smile.

'But a thought is still bothering me. Sin to sin, you were matching me! Then why were you so angry at my first offence of this kind!'

'Because I couldn't digest the fact that another woman could be more attractive to you than I am. One thought pinched me throughout the day, I wondered what I lacked!'

'They don't call women mysterious and unguessable for nothing! But I am curious to know what made you change your mind about leaving me at the last moment?'

Reeti's eyes become moist again. 'This is my home…and when it came to actually going away from it, I couldn't do it.'

'I see.'

'Anyway, in this whole drama, Lakshya is the real hero. His prank saved a marriage and terminated two clandestine affairs simultaneously. Otherwise, both of us were just biding our time, waiting to become full-fledged adulterers,' Reeti says as she continues to clasp his hand tightly.

'I agree with you. But there has been a side effect of this. I have become infamous as a womanizer. The irony is that I have been lecturing everyone to be ethical all this while.'

'Honestly, your skirt-chasing is not even thought of as crime by many. It is still a man's world. Amongst your friends and even your male relatives, you will be known as a stud. Ladies may blame me for not keeping you charmed enough. And there is some element of truth in this too. I may need a reality check. Get tips on "bed manners" from friends. Wear sexier lingerie and intoxicating perfumes.'

'You don't need to change one bit. In fact, I will become a typical Ludhianvi. I assure you that within a year, I will bring home a new Mercedes. But seriously, how do we limit the collateral damage?'

Reeti purses her lips. After thinking for a full minute, she speaks. 'I will fix this. Tomorrow, I will put up a humorous post on various social media platforms about how our son misread a forwarded WhatsApp post—and not a personal message—and caused a temporary rift between us.'

'Smart idea. But how will I dump the "other woman" and how will you kick out the "other man". They may be madly in love.'

'Oh, I never thought of that.'

And both of them bury their heads in their hands.

Jai Ludhiana! Jai Mercedes!